"I'LL HAVE YOU KNOW I once fancied myself very much in love. Back when I was a green girl. And he loved me!" Gilly said defiantly.

A small smile quirked the corners of Lord Marlowe's mouth. "But did he ever kiss you?"

She looked up, startled to find herself suddenly so close to him. "Of course not! He had too much respect for me."

"What a slow-top. It is fortunate I am so lacking in respect," he said, drawing her unresisting body into his arms, "because it is clearly past time." His mouth descended on hers with a thoroughness that left in no doubt that he considered she had indeed reached her majority. She could hear his heart beating through the clothing that separated them, feel his arms about her in a way that was positively possessive, as his hot mouth came down on hers. It seemed to brand and search her, and she knew she should fight, scream, or faint, that some resistance was definitely called for. She decided she could always blame the champagne, and entwined her arms about his neck, answering his mouth to the best of her limited experience.

That devastating kiss seemed to go on forever, and yet was far too short. He pulled back, looking down at her with a tender, mocking smile. "Not bad for a first attempt," he said huskily.

# Other Anne Stuart books from Bell Bridge Books

## Historical Romance

Prince of Magic

The Houseparty

Lady Fortune

The Demon Count Novels

Barrett's Hill

## Romantic Suspense

Nightfall

Shadow Lover

Now You See Him

The Catspaw Collection

# The Spinster and the Rake

by

## Anne Stuart

Bell Bridge Books

This is a work of fiction. Names, characters, places and incidents are either the products of the author's imagination or are used fictitiously. Any resemblance to actual persons (living or dead), events or locations is entirely coincidental.

Bell Bridge Books
PO BOX 300921
Memphis, TN 38130
Print ISBN: 978-1-61194-709-0

Bell Bridge Books is an Imprint of BelleBooks, Inc.

A mass market edition of this book was published by Dell Publishing Co., Inc. in 1982

We at BelleBooks enjoy hearing from readers.
Visit our websites
BelleBooks.com
BellBridgeBooks.com
ImaJinnBooks.com

10 9 8 7 6 5 4 3 2 1

Cover design: Debra Dixon
Interior design: Hank Smith
Photo/Art credits:
Garden(manipulated) © Unholyvault | Dreamstime.com
Couple (manipulated) © HotDamn Stock

:Lras:01:

# Dedication

In loving memory of Bill and Hildegarde. For Bill, who taught me so much. And Hildegarde, who gave me shelter from the storm.

# Chapter One

THERE WAS A heavy rain falling on the dusty, dry road between Winchester and London. The parched, rutted road drank the moisture in thirstily for a few moments, then tired of the bounty and sullenly gave over the potholes to the rapidly collecting rain. A crack of thunder, a jolt as the ancient landau hit a water-filled rut, and the dark-clad woman was thrown roughly to the side of the carriage. She was traveling alone, as she had for the past two years, and allowed herself the luxury of a good, solid, English "damn."

It had been a long day for Gillian Redfern, a spinster one month shy of thirty years of age. She usually alternated her days between the households of her two sisters and her elder brother. She was between siblings at the moment, traveling from her sister Pamela's house outside Winchester back to her brother's formidable mansion in Berkeley Square. As Pamela's husband, the ill-mannered and impossibly boorish Baron Sinford, was as purse-pinched as he was lecherous, Gillian had been allotted a very poor carriage indeed, usually reserved for transporting under-housemaids to the tooth-drawer, Gillian told herself with grim amusement, putting a hand to her aching head. Surely the thing must have been designed to accentuate all the bumps and lumps in the British roadway system. It wouldn't have been quite so bad if Pamela had allowed her to leave in decent time, instead of holding her back with all sorts of last-minute deputations to brother Derwent and then sending her off with a positively lethargic coachman and four of the laziest slugs that ever attempted to pass as decent quality horseflesh. It was no wonder they were hours late already, and Gillian's stomach was rumbling ominously. Pamela hadn't thought to send a picnic hamper either, and Gillian hadn't asked.

The youngest of the four children of a wealthy but unimaginatively proper gentleman, Gillian had long since decided, with a great deal of persuasion from the aforementioned siblings, to immolate herself on the altar of duty, having a great deal of family feeling and a dislike of being useless. Therefore, despite what amounted to an easy competence left to her by the good graces of a bluestocking maiden aunt and her mother's last defiant gesture, she spent her days chasing around after a singularly ill-assorted parcel of nieces and nephews, ran errands for her sisters, made up a fourth at whist though she despised the game, partnered the most tedious of necessary gentlemen guests at dinner, and listened to her brother's pontifications concerning the desperate state of the world, all brought about by a lenient attitude toward the Corsican monster and a preponderance of liberal-minded, wishy-washy bleeding hearts who hadn't the sound business sense or pride in their country. . . . At this point Gillian invariably allowed her thoughts to drift.

The rain was coming down in earnest now, pelting the sides of the carriage and making the slippery roadway even more treacherous. The coachman, who had heretofore been adamant in setting a snail's pace, must have decided that he didn't care for rain running down his collar, for the landau sped up with a jerk that sent Gillian tumbling back against the threadbare seats once more, uttering a second, satisfactory "damn."

To make the wretched situation complete, a leak had developed in the faded roof of the carriage, directly above Gillian's aristocratic Redfern nose. Large drops were descending with cheerful regularity, soaking her sober felt bonnet and trickling down the front of her navy wool spencer.

Gillian Redfern, usually a gentle and conciliatory creature, had a temper when aroused, and a hearty dislike of carriage accidents. She reached out a well-shaped, unjeweled hand and rapped sharply on the roof. "Slow down!" she shouted through the pelting rain. A sharp crack of the horseman's whip was the only answer vouchsafed, and the velocity increased. Gillian knocked more sharply. "Slow down!" she cried out. "We'll have an accident!"

With those fateful words barely out of her mouth an especially large pothole presented itself beneath the left leader's hoof. The horse stumbled, righted itself, and with a great deal of expertise never evinced before or after in his professional life, the coachman was able to lessen the rocking and swaying of the ancient landau. He had almost succeeded in getting the cumbersome thing under control when another, smaller carriage appeared out of nowhere, traveling at a tremendous pace, and chose just that moment to try to pass the Redfern carriage.

It was too much, for the frightened and exhausted horses, the overtaxed coachman, and the landau's rear axle. The first reared, the second dropped the reins, and the third snapped, sending the abused carriage with its unfortunate occupant hurtling off the road, landing on its side in the ditch.

The coachman, being in actuality one of Baron Sinford's more expendable grooms, immediately forgot about his passenger and looked first to the condition of the horses. Despite the animals' ages Baron Sinford disliked any of his possessions suffering harm, and it was with great relief that, upon closer inspection, the hapless coachman ascertained that the four seemed to have suffered more from fright than any actual damage.

"Are you all right, man?" A well-bred voice came out of the darkness, followed by its owner, who was nothing more than an extraordinarily tall shadow in the pelting rain.

"Fine, sir."

The first gentleman was joined by another, smaller shadow, and three pairs of hands released the horses' reins with deft speed.

"Now, my good man," the taller of the two said in a pleasant drawl, "you might tell me what the bloody hell you mean by driving all over the road like that! A glass or two to warm you on a damp night like this is all well and fine, but not when you're traveling the king's highway and endangering other travelers as well." This was all delivered in a mild tone, which didn't prevent it from being a blistering attack. And the coachman's very correct suspicion that his censor had also been imbibing with a free hand that evening didn't help matters. Ah, but it didn't do to argue with the gentry, and he *had* been taking a few too many sips out of his flask that Bessie had so thoughtfully provided, knowing full well that Mr. Derwent Redfern would begrudge a poor, weary groom a drop of something to warm his chilled bones.

"It's a lucky thing for you," the gentleman continued in that same gentle, pleasing voice, "that my coachman is such a damned good driver, and that you weren't carrying any passengers. Heaven knows what—"

"Oh, my God," the coachman gasped, staring transfixed at the silent bulk of the upended coach. "But I was."

At that moment the carriage door was pushed open from beneath, and a dark, bedraggled figure appeared in the pouring rain like a drowning jack-in-the-box. "Coachman?" she inquired in slightly subdued tones.

"Good heavens, it's a lady," the shorter gentleman exclaimed. "Who would have thought it, my dear Marlowe? You have all the luck. No doubt she'll be a stunner."

"Do shut up, Vivian," the taller figure said pleasantly, reaching the side of the carriage. "May I help you alight, ma'am? I trust you aren't injured?"

Gillian stared down at the pair in the darkness, trying to make out their faces in the pelting rain. By their voices they were well-bred, but in truth she had no option, other than standing half in and half out of a lopsided carriage in the pouring rain. A sharp crack of thunder decided her. "No, I'm not hurt, sir. Merely a trifle shaken up. I would appreciate some assistance in quitting this wretched landau."

"Certainly, ma'am." Before she could reach back into the carriage for her reticule an exceedingly strong pair of hands reached up around her, caught her elbows with a masterful grip, and pulled her out of the carriage with remarkable dispatch. As he set her down on the rain-soaked road, she stumbled slightly, and he reached out to steady her, his face shrouded by the wide-brimmed hat he wore. He was quite monstrously tall, she noticed, and couldn't help but be glad of it, considering that she stood five feet eight in her stocking feet.

"Good gad, you've plucked yourself a handful," the second gentleman observed with malicious cheer. "How do you manage, my dear Marlowe?"

Gillian was soaking wet, and aching in places a lady wouldn't admit existed. She spoke up with some asperity. "He obviously manages better than you do, sir, but I take leave to tell you that I'm no stunner, as you so charmingly put it. I am merely an extremely wet female seeking nothing so much as my home and my bed."

"Yes, ma'am." The gentleman accepted his reprimand with good humor unimpaired, his cheery voice somewhat slurred. "I beg pardon, miss. Hadn't meant to be offensive. Ask Marlowe there, he'll tell you. Harmless, I am, completely harmless."

"A complete fool is more like it. And the least we can do is see that Miss . . ." The tall gentleman waited for Gillian to supply the missing name, and when she failed to do so continued smoothly, "that Miss Incognita reaches her home and bed in short order. Madame, my coach awaits." He gave a courtly little bow, just slightly ironical, and Gillian considered him in the pouring rain.

Normally the very idea of accepting a ride alone in a carriage with a pair of strange gentlemen would be unacceptable. But surely, at a few weeks short of thirty, she was being tiresomely missish even to hesitate. It wasn't as if she were just out of the schoolroom, for heaven's sake.

"You are very kind," she accepted in what she hoped was a brisk, businesslike tone of voice. "If you're sure it will be no trouble?"

"No trouble at all," the tall gentleman said, his strong, possessive hand reaching under her left elbow and steering her toward his waiting carriage. "But I'm afraid you'll have to give up your anonymity. We can hardly convey you to your home if you don't tell us where it is."

"Berkeley Square," she said briefly, allowing him to help her into the small, light carriage. He and his companion followed her, and in the dim lamplight Gillian and the tall man referred to as Marlowe surveyed each other.

She was a fairly unprepossessing sight in the twilight of the small, well-sprung carriage. Past her first youth, without question, and never more than passably pretty in the first place, with that pale, narrow face shaded by the damp, unfortunate bonnet. The eyes were large and quite good, Marlowe thought impartially, and he suspected the mouth could curve up in an enchanting smile when she was feeling more at ease. To be sure, the nose was a trifle aristocratic for his tastes, since he had a partiality for snub noses, and she was too tall for fashion. But there was something indefinably appealing about her. He found himself wondering if her eyes were blue.

The coach started forward smoothly, without the jerk Gillian had become accustomed to with the constant succession of inferior coachmen that had been her recent lot in life. "Where in Berkeley Square?" Marlowe probed gently. "Come now, don't be worried. I don't think your employer will be too terribly harsh with you. After all, it was his fault you were out on a night like this."

Gillian stared covertly at the two gentlemen, wishing she'd had time to get a good look at them before the coach had started on this breakneck pace. She might have thought twice about her precipitous decision.

The shorter man, Vivian, Marlowe had called him, was bad enough. His round, cheery face was a bright red, the eyes bloodshot and watery and quite sly, the pate prematurely bald, revealing a high domed forehead wreathed with wrinkles. There were deep pouches beneath the eyes, a double chin, and a positive leer on the loose lips. He could have been anywhere between twenty and sixty, and he smelled strongly of brandy. And yet, of the two, he filled her with less trepidation.

While Marlowe removed his rain-soaked hat and leaned back against the squabs opposite her, Gillian was busy experiencing a novel situation. From the top of Marlowe's curly head, black locks liberally streaked with gray, past the cynical dark eyes surrounded by tiny lines of dissipation, and just possibly laughter, the sallow complexion of one who has spent a great many years in sunnier climes than Britain, the strong nose, and cynical, alarmingly attractive mouth, he was truly, wickedly appealing. Like his companion his age was difficult to judge, although Gillian estimated he was somewhere about forty. She also guessed, with great accuracy, that she was in the presence of a rake. Having been sheltered from and warned against those wicked creatures all her life, she viewed her deliverer with trepidation not unmixed with fascination.

"Have I grown another nose?" he inquired affably. "I've never been stared at so long or so intently before. Have we met?"

"I don't believe so," Gillian said, lowering her fascinated gaze hastily to her drab navy blue lap. She would scarcely have forgotten such a dangerously attractive face had she seen it.

"I would have been greatly surprised if we had," Marlowe agreed. "Considering that I've been out of the country for the last twenty years, you would have still been in leading strings when I left. Allow me to introduce myself. Ronan Patrick Blakely at your service. This is my friend, Vivian Peacock, who is also anxious to oblige. And you are . . . ?"

Still Gillian hesitated. This handsome, dissipated gentleman in front of her was doubtless some sort of black sheep, a remittance man come to haunt his aristocratic family like a proverbial bad penny. His friend called him Marlowe, which suggested a title, though the gentleman's casual manner didn't substantiate such an idea. She tried to remember what she knew of the Blakelys and seemed to recall a particularly stuffy, ancient marquis named Marlowe. They wouldn't like the charming reprobate opposite her, not one bit.

"You needn't worry that they'll turn you off without a character, my dear Miss Incognita," he continued smoothly. "I'm certain after twenty years my scandalous reputation will have paled noticeably. Your employers will scarcely look at me twice."

"Doing it a little too brown, Marlowe," Vivian snickered.

Marlowe ignored him. "Come, come. We can scarcely leave you off in the middle of Berkeley Square in the pouring rain, can we? Which house is your destination?"

There was no help for it, Gillian decided, still loath to disclose her actual relationship with the house in question. For one thing, she was hideously embarrassed that she should be mistaken for a governess or whatever it was they supposed her to be; for another, the less these two wicked-looking gentlemen knew about her, the better. "The Redfern mansion on the west side of the square," she admitted.

Marlowe let out a low whistle. "My dear girl, I am afraid that does complicate matters. Do you belong to the household of Derwent Redfern?"

"I do."

"I was afraid of that. I must confess that Mr. Redfern and I were never very close. A disagreement over a lady."

"It would be, knowing you," Vivian piped up. "Though what that dull stick Redfern would be doing in the petticoat line is beyond me."

"You forget, Viv, that it was twenty years ago."

"Who won?" Gillian was aghast to find herself asking. Her unruly tongue had caused her more than her share of trouble in the past twenty-nine years, and seemed determined to continue its work. She blushed.

Marlowe smiled at her, his practiced rake's smile, she told herself sternly, fighting its insidious attraction. "Need you ask?" he questioned without the slightest trace of vanity. "I could hardly expect that you'd be fond of the old boy. A more stiff-rumped cod's head I've never met . . ."

"Beg the lady's pardon, Marlowe," Vivian said blearily. "Mustn't use the term stiff-rumped in a lady's presence. Though come to think of it, don't know whether she's a lady or not. Very tricky situations, these governess-companions. Never know whether they're servants or gentry. Deuced embarrassing, at times. Especially when you're trying to give some fetching young thing a slip on the shoulder, and she turns out to be a poor relation. You'd best watch yourself, Marlowe. Redfern might have his eye on her already. A bit long in the tooth, you might say, but she ain't bad-looking. Ain't bad-looking at all. Besides, you should see what Letty Redfern's become. Fat as a pig, and just as smug as her spouse. Yes, you'd best watch yourself with Miss Incognita there. Don't be getting ideas that could run you into trouble all over again. Need to re-establish yourself. No seducing proper young ladies. Got to be careful." With that last utterance Vivian Peacock succumbed to the night's brandy and began to snore gently.

Once more that devastating smile was directed toward Gillian. "You'll have to excuse poor Vivian. He drank a bit too much tonight. Of course, he wasn't to know we'd have the honor of a lady's company."

"I thought it was yet to be determined whether or not I was a lady," Gillian shot back, amazed at her temerity. But if truth be told, she felt completely removed from her normal, humdrum life, bouncing over the nighttime roads in a carriage with the most attractive man she had ever seen in her life, bar none. The pouring rain drumming down on the carriage roof added to her sense of dreamlike isolation, where for once in her life she couldn't be called to account for her actions. They thought she was some sort of upper servant, and considering the limited circle of her acquaintance nowadays, there was no reason why they ever needed to find out otherwise. She could sit here in the darkness and be as pert as she pleased, as outspoken as she had always longed to be, and the wretched Derwent would never find out and deliver one of his thundering scolds. She met Marlowe's swarthy face with a smile of her own.

He blinked, startled. She was even prettier than he had anticipated when she smiled like that. A little flirtation would beguile the remainder of the trip, he decided. "Much as it grieves me to admit it, there's little doubt you're a lady, born and bred," he said mournfully.

"Why does it grieve you to admit it?" she inquired curiously.

"Because if you weren't it would enable me to make all sorts of outrageous suggestions."

Gillian smiled. "I wouldn't have thought you'd let someone's position in society stop you."

"It wouldn't, if they were married. But I make it a practice not to dally with single young women. I prefer 'em experienced." He was busy wondering how he was going to maneuver himself onto the seat beside her.

"Isn't that rather unfair? How can the poor ladies gain experience if you're going to be so harsh?" This was dangerous, and she knew it, but exhilaratingly so, and she couldn't resist.

That was more than enough invitation for a man of Marlowe's address. Before Gillian could gather her scattered wits he was sitting beside her, dangerously close, as Vivian slumbered on. "I could always be persuaded," he drawled in a beguiling undertone, "to make an exception or two."

Like a skittish mare Gillian slid out of his grasp, moving to the far side of the coach. Unfortunately she hadn't far to travel, and even hugging the door she was still ominously close. "Or two?" she questioned, her voice a brave quaver, wondering if she could bring herself to kick him.

He surveyed her for a long moment, his eyes alight with something she couldn't read. "One exception might be quite enough," he allowed, and reached for her.

# Chapter Two

"MR. MARLOWE . . ." she stammered nervously, practically cowering, her eyes wide and frightened in the dim light of the rocking carriage.

Vivian Peacock raised his balding head and eyed the two of them owlishly, not a trace of surprise at the change in seating arrangements marring his slightly dazed features. "Actually, he's Lord Marlowe, y'know," he confided. "Marquis of Herrington, what's more. Never saw a fellow so surprised when it turned out he was the heir. Thought your demmed uncle would live forever, didn't you, old boy? Never thought your cousin would pop off like that, either. Damned unhealthy, these wars. Wouldn't be caught dead in one." He chuckled softly to himself with pleasure over his little joke.

"Go back to sleep, Viv," the marquis ordered gently, his eyes still intent on Gillian's face.

"Heavens, no, m'boy. That would be rude," Vivian protested, pulling himself upright. "Forty winks, that was all I needed, and now I feel right as a trivet. As I was saying, Miss Whatchamacallit, here we had Ronan Patrick Blakely, black sheep of the Marlowe family, racketing around the Continent with pockets to let, and what happens? He gets the nod and returns home in triumph. To the bosom of your family, eh what?"

Marlowe had by this time accepted the inevitable with good grace, and he leaned back against the squabs, his broad shoulders inches away from Gillian, the predatory look in his eyes replaced by one of amusement. "I hadn't noticed any particular warmth in their welcome, Viv. As a matter of fact, you're the only one who was noticeably glad to see me."

"Well, of course, old man. We've been friends forever. It was the least I could do," Vivian said benignly, his bleary eyes going from the amused face to the nervous expression of their guest. "I say, did I interrupt anything?"

To Gillian's intense discomfiture Lord Marlowe laughed. "Nothing at all. I was merely about to demonstrate to Miss Incognita the difference between Derwent Redfern and my humble self."

"Didn't I warn you about toying with the lower orders? Especially this damned bourgeois class," Mr. Peacock reproved. "If I were you, Miss Thingummybob, I wouldn't get my hopes up. Lord Marlowe, I regret to inform you, is a rake."

"No!" cried Gillian in tones of mock amazement, having gathered her courage and her wits. "Surely you are too harsh."

"No, I swear." He leaned forward in drunken earnestness. "He may seem the jolliest of fellows, and indeed he is. Can't think of anyone I'd rather share a tipple with, or place a wager, or do just about anything. But he's a ladies' man. They all take one look at him and the world's well lost. Don't know how he does it, but you mark my words." He squinted at her in the darkness. "Now I know that you're not at all in his common line. But that doesn't mean you'd be safe. Believe me, Miss Thingummybob, he's—"

"She believes you, Viv," Marlowe drawled pleasantly. "And now that my character has been sufficiently blackened, I was hoping we might persuade our unwilling guest to disclose her name. Considering that we are now stopped outside the Redfern residence and an extremely angry gentleman is peering at us from the front door, we might—"

"Oh, merciful heavens!" Gillian said ruefully, scrambling for the door handle. A large, strong brown hand closed over hers, and she felt a thrill not unlike a shock as together they opened the door. Before she could leap out he moved, climbing down from the carriage with a grace illuminated by the streetlight, and reached out to help her down. The streetlights also illuminated Derwent Redfern's discontented, peevish face from the wide oak doors, and for a craven moment Gillian considered denying all knowledge of the house and requesting her rescuers to drive on. But there was no help for it, and sighing, she placed herself in those immeasurably strong hands that lingered just a touch too long at her slender waist. When he finally released her, she looked up, way up, into his face and was surprised by the amused understanding there.

"He's waiting for you," he said gently.

"I know." Her voice sounded unhappy to her own ears. "Perhaps you'd better just leave, and I'll explain . . ."

"I wouldn't think of it." He took possession of her arm and led her reluctant figure up the broad front stairs that were still slippery from the rain. "Not that he'll be particularly happy to see me, but despite Viv's aspersions on my character, I do not escort a *lady* home"—there was a sweetly mocking emphasis on the word—"and then leave her on the street. You get delivered into Redfern's hands, much as I think it a wretched fate."

The expression on her brother's face was enough to give pause to stouter souls than Gillian. But somehow the strong arm beneath her hand, the tall presence by her side lent her courage, and she lifted her head bravely and met Derwent's horrified eyes as they reached the top steps.

"Good evening, Redfern," Lord Marlowe greeted him smoothly, with just a trace of irony in his voice. "I have returned something to you."

With a curt nod Derwent acknowledged the taller man's greeting. "Marlowe," he said coolly. "I heard you were back in town." His tone of voice made it obvious that he hadn't greeted that news with any particular delight.

To Gillian's intense discomfiture he turned his chilly, condemning attention to her as she cowered beside Marlowe's tall, protecting figure. "And I might ask, my dear Gillian, how you happened to find yourself alone and unchaperoned with a gentleman of Lord Marlowe's reputation?"

"Derwent!" she exclaimed, so astounded by his rudeness that she failed to remember that Marlowe thought her an upper servant. She felt Marlowe's interested gaze on her flushed face, and cursed her too-ready tongue.

"There's no use looking so shocked, my girl," Redfern snapped. "If it got around that my sister was alone with a man like Ronan Blakely . . ."

"At no time at all was your sister alone with me, my dear Redfern." Marlowe seemed to take the relationship in stride. "If you would care to stroll down the front steps, you will find Vivian Peacock awaiting me in the carriage."

"There's not much to choose between the two of you," Derwent sniffed.

Marlowe sighed wearily. "If I had the time, my dear boy, I would love to teach you some manners. However, I really do dislike making a scene on the front steps with the servants around. And I resent your insulting attitude toward your sister, and most of all, I resent your pompous presence on this earth, but I doubt I'll bother doing anything to remedy the situation. Not tonight, at least." He took Gillian's chilled hand in his and brought it to his lips. "Your servant, Miss Redfern."

With a trace of defiance toward her sputtering brother, she met Marlowe's enigmatic gaze with a polite smile. "Thank you for rescuing me, Lord Marlowe. I am certain when I acquaint my brother with the details of this evening he will both apologize and thank you himself."

"All the details?" he questioned in a laughing under-voice that just missed Derwent's sharp ears. "I may have to meet him after all."

For some reason, despite her brother's ferocious glower and her intense dislike of scenes, Gillian found she could laugh. "Good evening, Lord Marlowe," she said emphatically, giving him a gentle shove in the direction of the carriage.

"Your servant, Redfern." He bowed and ran down the steps two at a time. As he reached the carriage a very drunken Vivian leaned out and waved blearily at the couple in the doorway. The result was not quite felicitous, but Gillian, taking her brother's unwilling arm in hers, said brightly, "You see, we were ably chaperoned the entire time. And if it weren't for Pamela's husband being so abominably pinchpenny as to send me out in a carriage that was falling apart, with the most wretchedly inept coachman and the saddest team of horses you have ever seen, I would have been fine. You are lucky I am not lying dead in some ditch between here and Winchester."

Derwent closed the door behind them, his narrow, unpleasant face full of condemnation. "Have you ever heard the phrase, dear sister, 'death before dishonor'?"

Handing her rain-soaked felt hat and pelisse to an avidly listening servant, she stripped off her gloves. "I have hardly been dishonored, brother dear, and no one would be likely to think so if you would only desist in these dire predictions."

Against her will Gillian found her elbow grasped in Derwent's rough grip, and she was thrust into the drawing room. The door slammed shut behind her. Despite the dampness of the spring evening it was quite warm, but Derwent, who always complained bitterly of drafts, had caused a roaring fire to be built. The result was something closer to the tropics than London on a spring evening. Gillian's wool dress began to steam gently.

Taking a seat well away from the blaze, she eyed Derwent with an air of resigned expectation that just bordered on irritation. For some reason she felt less willing to deal with Derwent's moral posturings than usual.

"Do you have any idea," he began, placing his stubby fingertips together in a meditative pose, "just how bad Lord Marlowe's reputation is?"

"Mr. Peacock was good enough to enlighten me," she replied flippantly. "What would you have had me do, Derwent? The rear axle on the carriage broke. It was dark and raining. Should I have stayed in an overturned carriage till morning instead of accepting Lord Marlowe's very civil offer of help?" she demanded with a certain amount of heat. "And you haven't even thought to ask me whether I've taken any harm from the mishap. You've been too busy ranting on about my precious reputation to care for any bodily ills. As if such fustian would matter with a woman my age. I may remind you that I am not a helpless schoolroom chit. I am a spinster of advanced years, and hardly the easy prey of a . . . a . . ."

"A rake," Derwent supplied, staring at his sister in surprise. "I must say, Gillian, this attitude of yours astounds me. You've always trusted my judgment in these matters before. Lord Marlowe is doubtless a very appealing fellow. Most rakes are. But the Redferns have also been rather high sticklers, and it wouldn't do for us to associate with all the riffraff prevalent in the ton nowadays."

"You call a marquis 'riffraff'?"

"This particular one I do. To be sure, the Blakelys are an old, respected family, almost as old as the Redferns. But the current incumbent is nothing more than a wastrel. He was sent abroad by his family when he was no more than twenty. Something to do with a female, of course."

"What about a female?" she asked curiously.

"Really, Gillian, I am not about to sully your ears with such a sordid tale. Take my word for it, the lady in the situation was married, but Marlowe, or Ronan Blakely as he was then, was old in the ways of sin, despite his lack of years. And it was not his first offense. His poor family had no option but to pension him off. It is most unfortunate that he should have come into the title, most unfortunate indeed. We shall have to be polite, of course, but that is as far as it will go, Gillian. Tomorrow I shall draft a very polite note thanking him for his assistance to my sister, and that will be the end of it. I do realize, my dear," he continued in a kinder tone that set Gillian's nerves on edge, "that despite your maturity of years you are still quite innocent. As it should be in a maiden lady. In lieu of a husband it is my duty to stand as protector to you, to warn you from undesirable acquaintances and to keep fortune hunters away."

"I am entirely able to choose my own acquaintances, Derwent," she said in a mild tone.

"Of course, you are," he agreed with an indulgent laugh. "And I know I can trust your good judgment in being guided by me in these matters. Come, don't let us argue any further. It is good to have you back. Letty and Felicity missed you, and the children were impossible. I do not understand why they refuse to mind anyone but you. You have been sorely missed."

A pair of mocking eyes slowly faded from Gillian's wistful memory, as she prepared to face her next round of duties. "And I have missed them," she said dutifully, if with slightly less enthusiasm than she usually showed.

In the meantime Ronan Patrick Blakely, Lord Marlowe, the sixth marquis of Herrington, was making abstracted answers to Vivian Peacock's whiskey-laden inanities as they barreled through the rain-soaked, deserted London streets toward Blakely House on Bruton Street. Had they been traveling directly, they would have been home in less than a minute, Blakely House being adjacent to the Redfern town house. But by carriage the path was particularly convoluted, giving Mr. Peacock more than enough time to observe his lordship's distracted air.

"See here, Marlowe, you ain't interested in that bit of muslin, are you? She hardly seems in your line at all," he protested.

Lord Marlowe gave his companion his singularly sweet smile. "You mistake the matter, Viv. Miss Incognita was none other than Derwent Redfern's sister."

This was surprising enough almost to sober Mr. Peacock. "Gammon! I've met both his sisters. One's a great horsey creature in Kent, the other's a regular out and outer. This one doesn't fit either description."

"I gather this is a third sister. One who never married."

"An ape-leader, eh? I warned you she'd be trouble if you trifled with her, Ronan, my boy."

Lord Marlowe was leaning back against the cushions, eyeing the dark sky with the rain clouds scudding fitfully about. "I have no intention of trifling with her, Viv," he said mildly, apparently engrossed in the view.

"That's not to say. . . . Well, perhaps I should keep my mouth shut," Vivian said. "But I wonder . . ."

"What do you wonder?"

"Whether she could fall under the fabled Marlowe charm? Do you ever fail, Ronan?" he asked with simple curiosity.

"Not if I put my mind to it."

"It would be entertaining if you were to have Derwent Redfern's maiden sister infatuated with you. Rather nice revenge, don't you think?"

"No, I don't think so," Marlowe replied sharply.

"But it was Redfern who managed to get you sent away so long ago. He spread that particularly foul rumor about, didn't he?"

"It was. Derwent Redfern, not his innocent sister, Viv."

Vivian cocked a sly eye at him. "Are these scruples I hear coming from my old friend? I know the problem. You doubt your infallible charm. You know there's no way you could bring a Redfern under your spell."

Marlowe hesitated for only a moment, having imbibed a great deal of brandy himself not too long ago, and being disturbingly haunted by a pale face and a beguiling smile. "Would you care to place a wager that I couldn't?"

"What amount were you thinking on?"

Marlowe smiled seraphically. "A thousand pounds, Viv?"

"Done! I have little doubt it'll do the poor girl good. Imagine having Derwent Redfern for a brother!" Vivian shuddered. "But I'm counting on her to hold out. I'll watch your progress with interest, my boy."

Marlowe smiled a slow, sensual smile. "So shall I, Viv. So shall I."

# Chapter Three

IT WAS AN exceedingly attractive family tableau in the upper withdrawing room in Berkeley Square. Gillian sat far removed from the sweltering fire, her dark blue dress unbuttoned at the top, her reddish-blond hair pinned neatly back, her blue eyes surveying her family with tolerant affection.

Her sister-in-law, Letty Wilberforce Redfern, was curled up by the fire, her moon face flushed with the heat, one plump hand moving from the chocolate box to her mouth with monotonous regularity. Her daughter, as slender and delicate as her mother was plump, strode around the room, bursting with her customary energy, her dark eyes flashing, her high cheekbones flushed. There was little question that Miss Felicity Redfern was one of the nonpareils of the season. With her clouds of midnight black hair, the delicate nose, rosebud mouth, and creamy white skin, she found that very few could find fault with such perfection. Certainly not her doting relatives. Fortunately Felicity was as kindhearted as she was beautiful. She was also as high-spirited, which, according to her parents, was not quite so fortunate. "Just like her Aunt Gillian before she settled down," was the usual judgment, and her Aunt Gillian would make a small moue of distaste at her present staid self.

"You will never guess what Bertie has told me," Felicity was in the midst of saying with a great deal of excitement, her dark eyes snapping. "The entire ton is talking."

"The entire ton is always talking about something or other," Gillian observed tranquilly. "And I don't know if it's at all the thing to be gossiping with your cousin. After all, he's supposed to be in London to sop up some learning, not to lead a rackety life."

"Stuff!" Felicity scoffed. "You're just trying to sound like Papa. You know you think they've treated poor Bertie abominably, sending him down for such a little prank."

"I'm persuaded your Aunt Gillian has far too much sympathy for Bertie," Felicity's mother put in in her customarily exhausted tones. "And you also know perfectly well that despite her high resolve, she enjoys a good bit of gossip just as much as you or I. What has Bertie told you?"

There was a question in Felicity's fine eyes as she surveyed her aunt, and Gillian gave a little nod, redirecting her own attention to the mending in her lap. Letty was always too tired to look after the mending, and Felicity too scatterbrained, so the bulk of the work usually went to Gillian. Mrs. Redfern was too high a stickler to entrust her fine laces to a servant's rough touch.

"It's about the new marquis of Herrington. Lord Marlowe, that is. Apparently he is setting up a gaming club."

"And what is so extraordinary about that?" Letty questioned peevishly. "I am persuaded any number of gentlemen have invested in such clubs, with no questions asked."

"But Lord Marlowe intends to do more than invest. He and Vivian Peacock are planning to run the place! Apparently Lord Marlowe ran a gambling hell when he was in Vienna, just before coming into the title, and he has said that he misses it!" Felicity surveyed her female relatives to gauge their reaction to this shocking piece of news.

"I don't expect he'll be received after such behavior," Letty observed comfortably.

"But that's where you're wrong, Mama. According to Bertie, all the gentlemen have professed themselves breathless with anticipation, and the majority of the ladies also. It is odd, isn't it," she mused, "how one gentleman can do something and be ostracized for it, and another can do the exact same thing and be applauded. I have come to the melancholy conclusion that society is both fickle and shallow," she announced.

"Such great wisdom for eighteen years of age," Gillian said cheerfully. "Whatever is left for such a worldly-wise young lady? A convent at best."

"Silly! I have no intention of abjuring the world. Not yet, at any rate. And I certainly wouldn't do it if I were still as young as you are, Gilly. I can think of any number of men who would be at your feet if you gave them half a chance."

"Your aunt doesn't care for parties and having men at her feet," Letty said sharply, forgetting her chocolates for the moment. "She's quite content as she is."

Gillian looked up from her mending, a smile in the fine eyes. "Thank you, Letty. It's always nice to be told when one is happy."

"Didn't you actually meet Lord Marlowe?" Felicity asked hastily, throwing her slender body down beside her aunt, causing Gillian to prick herself with her needle. "I gather he's terrifically handsome. I've simply been longing to meet him, but so far our paths haven't crossed. I don't suppose he'll be allowed in Almack's?"

"It would be extremely unlikely," Gillian allowed.

"Well, frankly I think it rather tame myself, so I wouldn't doubt he'd be just as happy not to have to go. Is he as handsome as they say he is?" she continued, ignoring her mother's look of displeasure. "Ginny Elverston says he makes shivers run up and down her spine when he just looks at her. Did he do that to you?"

"Certainly not!" Gillian lied unhesitatingly. "He's far too old for you, Felicity. Close to forty, I would imagine. As for being handsome, well, I suppose he is, though I didn't get that good a look at him. It was a dark, rainy night well over two weeks ago, and I am not certain I would even recognize him again if I were to see him. I am convinced *he* would not know me."

"And a good thing it is," Letty piped up. "Lord Marlowe is not the sort of person Redferns associate with. If we're forced to meet him we should be distantly polite, but that is all. Derwent says—"

"Don't you feel it's a trifle warm in here, Letty?" Gillian wondered hastily.

"Not in the slightest. Derwent says you've always been overheated. My fingers can be practically numb from the cold, and you suggest opening the windows! I trust you weren't about to make any such callous suggestion?"

"No, Letty," Gillian said meekly. "I thought Felicity and I might go for a walk. I need some new ribbons for my green dress, and the air would do us good."

"Derwent does not approve of that dress, Gillian," Letty said darkly. "Even with new ribbons. It's too young for you."

"That's as may be, but I happen to like it. The empire won't collapse if I wear a dress that is a trifle frivolous," Gillian replied with unimpaired good nature.

"I would love to go with you, Gilly," Felicity broke in quickly. "Is there anything we can get you, Mama?"

Letty leaned back against the cushions, resting her plump arm along the tufted back. "Nothing, dear. I believe I shall have to rest this afternoon. I am absolutely exhausted," she said in a plaintive voice. "If you do happen to pass the confectionary . . ."

"We'll get you some more chocolates," Felicity supplied cheerfully. "Of course, Mama. You get a rest. You mustn't overtire yourself."

"Someday," she confided to Gillian a short while later as they were strolling down the sidewalk, "she will get too lazy even to breathe."

Gillian laughed. "Unkind girl. Your brothers and sisters can be very exhausting, you know."

Felicity nodded her head beneath the fetching green creation, whose bill had sent her father into a screaming tantrum a few short days ago. "I know that perfectly well. Which is why she leaves them entirely in your care except for holidays and when guests arrive."

"Hardly in my care, Felicity. Nurse and Miss Hammersmith do a marvelous job," she said seriously. "But I didn't bring you out with me to discuss the children."

"I was afraid of that," Felicity said ruefully, her eyes downcast. "What have I done now?"

"Done?" echoed Gillian, startled. "I wasn't aware that you had done anything. Am I such an ogre that you always expect me to reprimand you?"

"No, of course not, best of all my aunts! And besides, I'd rather *you* take me down a peg or two than anyone else. You always make such sense when you do, and don't make a person feel like a loathsome worm or the most ungrateful creature alive. Bertie agrees with me—we both think you're a great gun."

Gillian was not impervious to flattery, but she had a goal in mind and refused to be distracted. "I wanted to ask you about Liam Blackstone."

Felicity's creamy complexion turned a deep rose that was scarcely less attractive. "Who told you?" she demanded in a strangled tone.

"I hardly think that matters," Gillian said gently.

"It does to me. I want to know who it is that I can't trust. Was it that little skunk Bertie? I should have known he'd rat on me the moment my back was turned."

"No, it wasn't Bertie. And I thought, dear Felicity, that you trusted *me*." The reproof was delivered in very gentle tones, but had the effect of making the younger girl look up at her aunt, completely stricken.

"Of course I trust you, Gilly. But I know how Papa terrorizes you, and I thought you would be better off not knowing. That way you wouldn't have to lie for me and feel miserable doing it."

"Very sacrificing of you, my dear," Gilly said with only the hint of a smile. "And you also remembered how I turn bright red when I lie, so that my brother knows immediately that something is up."

"That too," Felicity admitted, unabashed. "It must have been Marjorie who told you. She thinks just because she's been my maid forever she can interfere in my life. Well, she can't."

Gillian didn't trouble to deny it. "Marjorie was only worried about you, Felicity. As I am. Didn't your father order you not to see Mr. Blackstone again?"

"Yes."

"Then, though I can't say I'm surprised at your disobeying him, I *am* surprised at Liam Blackstone's being so unprincipled as to encourage you behind your father's back."

"He didn't!" Felicity shot back. "He hasn't encouraged me, not one tiny bit. He's always telling me to go away. He just doesn't mind that I go down to his mission whenever I can, and help him."

"To Stepney?" Gillian questioned faintly. "Do you realize how dangerous it is?"

"I realize it better than you, Gilly. And I don't mind. If Liam has chosen the poorest, dirtiest slum in London for his work, then there is nothing I'd rather do than help him. He lets me, sometimes. I've helped ladle out the soup for those poor unfortunates, and I've been trying to get Mrs Buddles to teach me how to cook. I am determined to be worthy of him, Gilly. And I will be."

Her aunt stared at her usually flighty young niece, and was touched. "You still love him." It was a statement, not a question.

"More than ever." There was a dignity about her, despite her extreme youth. "It's been three years since we met, nine months since Papa forbade me to see him. And every time I see him I love him more. I'm going to marry him, Gilly. I'm not going to let my family ruin my life as they did yours."

"My family did not ruin my life," Gillian said calmly.

"You spend your life watching other people's children," Felicity said cruelly.

"It was my choice."

Felicity eyed her aunt speculatively. "I don't know that I quite believe you," she said frankly. "But I do know that that sort of life is not for me. Neither is being married to a vicious lecher like Uncle Sinford, or a dull stick like Uncle Talmadge."

"I don't think either of them offered for you, my dear," Gilly pointed out with a trace of amusement.

"You know perfectly well what I mean. They're just the sort Redfern women marry. I would rather be a spinster than marry someone like that, and I would most of all prefer to marry Liam. If I could only persuade him." She wrinkled her fair brow as she pondered her problem, and Gillian resisted the impulse to reach out and smooth the cares away.

"Well, you will have to be a little more careful, my dear," she said instead in a prosaic tone of voice. "What I found out others can also discover."

Felicity caught her hand between hers, her dark eyes beseeching. "Then you won't tell my parents?"

"Tell them what? That you've done some charity work for the poor people in Stepney? I wouldn't think that would interest them all that much."

"Bless you, Gilly." Her voice throbbed with intensity.

"In the meantime, do you suppose we might go into the shop?" she inquired, merriment dancing in her blue eyes.

Felicity looked about her in surprise. "We're here already?"

"We've been standing outside Madame Racette's for the last five minutes, attracting no end of attention. If we might go in . . . ?"

THE MISSES REDFERN were some of Madame Racette's most honored customers, and Madame herself always waited upon them, no matter who else was at that moment enjoying her patronage. To be sure, Miss Gillian Redfern could never be persuaded to wear anything but drab grays and navy blues, all of the most depressing cut, but her taste was unerring when it came to the dressing of her beautiful young niece. Now there was a lady it was a pleasure to dress, not like some of the fat old harridans who came to her shop demanding dresses that were designed for girls twenty years younger and twenty pounds lighter.

And there had been a ray of hope where Miss Gilliam Redfern was concerned. Two weeks ago, upon returning from a visit to the country, she had unexpectedly chosen an absolutely charming dress in nile green, cut daringly low for Miss Redfern, though boringly high for most of Madame Racette's customers. Madame Racette had had visions of a complete transformation of the elder Miss Redfern's boring wardrobe, though such a grand order had yet to materialize. But hope sprang eternal, and when her assistant came to the private showing room and whispered of the Redferns' arrival, she made a hasty excuse to the saturnine gentleman and his companion and rushed from the room, promising to return momentarily.

"Ah, Mademoiselle Redfern!" she cried as she swept into the room, two mannequins in her choicest creations trailing along behind. "What an honor it is to see you this lovely spring afternoon. Is it too much to hope I might interest you in another dress? The one Babette is wearing I might have designed with you in mind. Such a color was made to be worn with hair such as yours. Notice the sweep of the skirt, the embroidered detail on the bodice." Madame Racette was too experienced a businesswoman to miss the light of covetousness that filled Gillian's blue eyes.

Gillian controlled her sudden longing. The dress was too young, the color, a soft aqua, was outrageous, and as for the cut—there was no bodice at all. She would look like a courtesan. "No, madame, I have not come for another dress," she said nobly, looking away. "I merely needed some ribbons to go with my last dress."

"Ribbons!" Madame dismissed them with an airy gesture. "Look at this dress, mademoiselle. It is you! Surely you cannot deny that you would look *ravissant* in it."

"I wouldn't deny it, but I also have no intention of purchasing such an indecent dress."

"Oh, Gillian, it's beautiful!" Felicity added her unwanted opinion. "You would look stunning in it, you know you would."

"Listen to your niece, mademoiselle. That one, she has the eye, just like you."

Gillian felt her conviction weaken. It was a monstrously attractive dress. "What is the price, madame?"

Quickly calculating the added prestige the sale would give her, she figured the cost of the gown, multiplied it by ten, subtracted five pounds, and named a staggering figure.

"That settles it, then. It is far too dear. The ribbons, madame," Gillian said firmly.

"But, Gillian, it would be so beautiful on you!" Felicity wailed. "You are mad to turn it down."

Gillian allowed herself one last covetous look. It would transform even the plainest creature into something close to beauty, she thought, and found herself wondering what a certain disreputable peer might think were he to be privileged to see Miss Gillian Redfern in such a glorious dress. Sternly she put that dangerously enticing thought from her mind. "Felicity, the dress is not for me."

"But that's where you're wrong," a gentle voice came from directly behind them, a voice surprisingly familiar, considering that Gillian had only heard it on one other occasion in her life, two short weeks ago. "I think the dress would be perfect for you, Miss Redfern."

With a feeling of anticipation that she told herself was embarrassment and dread, Gillian turned slowly to meet Ronan Marlowe's quizzical expression.

# Chapter Four

HER STARTLED BLUE eyes traveled up the seemingly endless length of him, to his saturnine face towering above her. In the brightly lit shop the streaks of gray in his curly black head stood out more prominently, as did the tiny lines around his eyes and mouth. He was dressed in great elegance, all in black, and on his hand was a large emerald, hard and cold and bright. Like his laughing green eyes.

Gillian felt her face flushing like a veritable schoolgirl, and silently cursed the man for having such a devastating effect on her. An effect he was no doubt well aware of. She met his amused glance firmly. "Good afternoon, Lord Marlowe. I was wondering when we might meet again."

"Were you, Miss Redfern? And I had rather thought you were avoiding me. Not that I blamed you, of course. I fancied I detected your brother's fell hand in the matter. I may have maligned him." The gentle voice drawled on, and Gillian had no doubt he was enjoying her discomfiture.

She threw back her head and met his gaze with a limpid one of her own. "Aren't you pleased you were mistaken, Lord Marlowe?" she asked brightly. "And speaking of Derwent, may I present you to his daughter, Felicity?" She turned to her companion and recognized the sparkling gaze with a sinking feeling. Despite Felicity's devotion to her stern vicar, she still had a penchant for attractive men, and Ronan Marlowe certainly fit that description. He seemed to have a devastating effect on the girl. She looked up at him, her dark eyes shining, lips parted breathlessly, cheeks flushed. Gillian hoped irritably that *she* hadn't looked like that when she saw him.

She could tell by the amused expression in those green eyes that Marlowe recognized Felicity's condition as he acknowledged the introduction with a courtly little bow that just bordered on mocking, and Felicity's answering smile, bright enough to dazzle a blind man, filled her with dread. What man could resist such loveliness? Certainly not a rake like Ronan Marlowe. Therefore it was with surprise that she found him turning back to her, all that magnetic attention focused on her until she felt almost faint.

"Are you going to buy that dress?" he demanded in a lazy voice. "It would suit you, you know."

"No, I don't know," Gillian lied. "And I have no intention of buying it. It would be completely unsuitable for me."

"Unsuitable for the role your family has pushed you into," he observed. "I can see how Derwent would want to keep you in such hideously drab clothes. He wouldn't want to lose his unpaid drudge." This was all delivered in such a mild tone of voice that Felicity, off to one side and staring at him dreamily, failed to notice.

Gillian stared at him, aghast. "How dare you?" she demanded. "What gives you the right . . . ?"

"Oh, I'm a very daring fellow," he replied easily. "If it's a simple matter of pockets to let, I would be honored to buy the dress for you."

There was a hiss of horrified reaction from the women around them, and even Gillian was temporarily silenced by the shocking suggestion. She forced herself to speak in calm, measured tones, only her becomingly flushed face betraying her agitation.

"I'm afraid I must decline your kind offer," she said stiffly. "I am entirely able to purchase that gown if by any chance I wished to. However, I do not." She bit back the blistering attack on his behavior that threatened to bubble over. By the light in his cool green eyes she knew perfectly well that he was entirely aware how outrageous his offer had been, and she wouldn't gratify him by ringing a peal over him as he so richly deserved.

He shrugged philosophically. "Well, if there's no persuading you we might as well leave."

"We?" she echoed, uneasiness warring with a treacherous spurt of pleasure.

"I am scarcely going to leave you to make your way home alone. I can't think why two lovely women thought it would be acceptable to go for a walk in the heart of London without a footman at least to accompany them. This is no longer the country, Miss Redfern."

"And you are such a stickler for the proper observances, aren't you, my lord?" she shot back pertly.

"That's my girl," he approved softly.

Once more Gillian cursed her flippant tongue. "But we wouldn't think of taking you away, Lord Marlowe. Though what a bachelor would be doing in an establishment such as Madame Racette's excites my curiosity, I must confess."

"Your curiosity will have to remain excited—I have no intention of telling you." He moved away and murmured something in a low voice in Madame Racette's attentive ear. That lady had watched the past few minutes' byplay with great fascination, and now accepted Marlowe's instructions with a complacent nod.

"I will inform the lady," she replied in a low voice that nevertheless reached Gillian's straining ears. She felt a very real temptation to stroll back to the private showing room from which Marlowe had so recently exited. She had never seen a wicked woman before, and would have been greatly interested to see the sort that Ronan Marlowe preferred. Before she could screw up her courage, however, Marlowe put one strong hand under her elbow, with a flirtatious and, for once, relatively silent Felicity on his other side, and a moment later they were strolling down the sidewalk at a leisurely pace, heading back toward Berkeley Square.

"What makes you think we've finished our shopping?" Gillian demanded crossly, hotly aware of the hand beneath her arm, her mind still lingering belatedly on the phrases "hideously drab clothes" and "unpaid drudge." If that was what he thought of her it was a wonder he even bothered to recognize her. Though perhaps the adoring creature on his right was the reason for his attentions. The thought depressed her even more. She would have to hint him away if that was what he had in mind. She didn't intend her Felicity to end up leg-shackled to a rake twice her age.

"I have not the slightest objection to escorting you further. I merely assumed since you came out without anyone to carry your purchases that you weren't planning a major shopping expedition. But if you wish . . ."

"Don't be difficult, Gilly." Felicity finally found her tongue. "I think it absolutely delightful of Lord Marlowe to escort us home. We can look in shop windows on the way, and perhaps we could persuade him to stop in for tea. Mama will be delighted to make his acquaintance."

"Your mother and I have been acquainted these twenty years," Marlowe said easily. "Since long before you were born. If I remember her correctly, she would be far too exhausted to support having uninvited guests drop in for tea. Instead, why don't you allow me to take you to Gunters for ices?"

Before Gillian could politely but firmly refuse, Felicity had clapped her hands together. "That would be delightful. And we could stop in that little jewelry store on the corner and pick up my locket. The man promised he'd have it mended by Tuesday, and here it is Friday already. How delightful that we ran into you, Lord Marlowe."

"Delightful," Gillian echoed gloomily, having just met the scandalized gaze of Letty's best friend across the street. The hand on her elbow squeezed slightly, and she looked up in surprise at the dark, lined, cynical face of her companion.

"Have I ruined you?" he asked softly with a meaningful glance in Mrs. Travers's horrified direction.

"It would take a great deal more than a chaperoned stroll in broad daylight with the infamous Lord Marlowe to ruin my reputation," she replied loftily.

"That bad, eh?" he commiserated. "Who'd have thought you'd be that hopelessly starched-up, that a rogue like me wouldn't discredit you. I can see I arrived in London just in time." There was an enigmatic promise in his eyes.

"I beg your pardon?"

He ignored her startled interjection. "Ah, well, I mustn't forget you're Derwent's sister. There must be some resemblance there, some sympathy of feeling."

"There is not!" She denied it hotly, knowing that he was teasing her but rising to the bait nonetheless. "Derwent and I have been at daggers drawn for as long as I can remember. But that doesn't mean I don't have a particle of sense, and know a . . . a . . ."

"Rake? A blunder, a degenerate cad?" he supplied amiably, his eyes alight.

"I didn't say that."

"No, but that's what you were thinking, wasn't it, my love? I take leave to tell you, my dear Miss Redfern, that I am accepted just about everywhere nowadays. I am a veritable pillar of society. You would hardly be so cruel as to deny a reformed rake such as me of your ennobling companionship?" The laughter in his voice was dangerously beguiling.

"Idiot!" She laughed reluctantly. "And I hadn't heard you were a reformed gambler."

"Am I not allowed to place a few wagers?" he questioned innocently. "Faith, but the Redferns are a sticky lot. I am not allowed to womanize or gamble if I'm to be admitted to their august company. Am I allowed to drink, or is that too denied me?"

"I don't doubt you drink too much," Gillian observed sternly.

"You are wise not to do so. I drink too much, gamble too much, and spend too much time and money on women who are no better than they should be." He smiled down at her, that lazy, beguiling smile that had such a dangerous effect on her. "And I chase shy, flustered young women who try to pretend they are aging spinsters well before their time."

"I'm going to be thirty in a matter of days," she cried, nettled. "And I am not a shy, flustered young woman."

"I didn't say I was chasing *you*," he said gently. "I merely make a habit of seeking out such blue-deviled females and cheering them up."

"Then you certainly aren't referring to me. I would scarcely call your attentions cheering," Gillian shot back. "They border on harassment."

"*Touché*," he said lightly. "I am so glad to see your eyes are blue. I had been hoping they would be, but everyone I asked during the last two weeks couldn't remember. I suppose it is because you usually keep them meekly downcast. You shouldn't, you know. They really are magnificent."

"You asked people what color my eyes are?" she demanded in horror. "You must be mad!"

"Merely eccentric. Is your hair red or blond? I still cannot see beneath that intimidating bonnet." He leaned down to peer at her earnestly, forcing a reluctant laugh from her.

"Behave yourself, Lord Marlowe. It's a bit of both."

"You should laugh more often," he observed, a thoughtful expression on his world-weary, handsome face. "It proves you aren't nearly as starched-up as you pretend to be. I don't despair of you yet."

"If you two would stop arguing," Felicity's aggrieved tones came to their startled ears, "I would appreciate it if someone would accompany me into the shop." There was just a suggestion of a pout on Felicity's pretty face. Being the pampered eldest daughter of doting parents, and an acknowledged toast, she wasn't used to being ignored by handsome men. Especially not for her beloved aunt, who, though Felicity adored her, was seen by her niece more in the light of a useful appendage for her own comfort, rather than another female and a possible rival for attention. The thought was obviously not a comfortable one.

"We will both be enchanted to accompany you, Miss Redfern," Marlowe said in that smooth, deep voice. "Lead the way."

It would have been too much to hope for Marlowe to behave himself in the jeweler's shop. He did stay reasonably in the background while Felicity pored over what seemed to Gillian's weary eyes every single piece of jewelry in the shop. It took all the tact Gillian possessed to steer her attention away from several inordinately gaudy pieces that Felicity had taken a fancy to. Likewise the flawed emerald ring, the pearls made of fish-paste, the ruby and sapphire earbobs that would have pulled down her ear lobes, and the gold bracelet that accompanied every move of Felicity's graceful arm with an annoying jangle.

"If you must buy some new jewelry," Gillian said wearily, "and I fail to see why you must, then why don't you consider that delightful little enamel locket over there? It has a delicacy and charm totally lacking in the brooch you're holding, as I'm sure you've already decided."

Felicity had been about to purchase the offending brooch, but immediately laid it down on the glass-topped counter. She knew far too well that her aunt's taste was unerring. "I already have several lockets," she stated. "Not that that's not pretty, though a trifle on the small side."

"Well, I like it," Gillian said strongly. "And if I weren't too old to be wearing lockets, I would buy it for myself. What about the diamond earbobs? They're small also, but quite lovely, and I don't believe you have any diamond earrings."

"I prefer colored stones." Felicity dismissed them, and Gillian allowed herself one last longing look at the earbobs.

"GUNTERS NEXT!" Felicity announced brightly as they stepped back out into the sunshine. "I declare I am famished."

Gillian looked toward Marlowe with a sinking expression, and he finally took pity on her. "I think your aunt wishes you to return home, Miss Redfern. These jaunts can be rather strenuous for someone of her advanced years. Perhaps another time."

The pout reappeared, less enchantingly this time. With practiced charm that positively enflamed Gillian with fury he reached down and pinched her niece's chin. "Now don't be difficult, child," he said gently. "Your aunt's had enough of me for one day."

"Well, I haven't," Felicity announced with unbecoming pertness.

Marlowe smiled his slow, delightful smile. "But I care more for your aunt's good opinion than I do for yours," he said, and led them inexorably down the street to the Redfern mansion, with Felicity fuming and Gillian completely bewildered. She stopped a few feet away from the imposing gray edifice that had housed Redferns in London for over a hundred years.

"I suppose you'd best leave us here," she said breathlessly. "Thank you for accompanying us. I do appreciate it."

"What a bouncer! You've been wishing me at the devil the entire time," he replied, looking down into those vulnerable blue eyes. "You want shaking up, Gillian. You're too complacent at too young an age."

A bitter little smile twisted her soft lips. "You're not as astute as I thought you were, Lord Marlowe, if you think I'm complacent. And I didn't give you leave to address me by my Christian name."

"No, you didn't," he agreed, taking her gloved hand in his and bringing it swiftly to his lips before she could pull away. "I'll let you escape this time, my love. I suppose I shouldn't blame you for being afraid of Derwent."

"I am not afraid of my brother!" She denied it hotly.

"No?" He was unconvinced, deliberately goading her. "You'll have to prove it to me at some later date, Gillian. Good afternoon, Miss Felicity."

Felicity's response was a distempered flounce, but Marlowe's tall back was already turned, and he was deprived of her temper. Gillian's troubled gaze followed him as he made his leisured way back down the square, back, no doubt, to Madame Racette's and the high-flyer he had left behind. Gillian was unaccountably disheartened.

Her niece let out a deep sigh, her pique vanishing. "He certainly is one of the most devastatingly attractive men I have ever seen," she announced soulfully. "Don't you agree, Gilly?"

"What about Liam Blackstone?" her aunt inquired with a trace of sharpness.

"Oh, Liam's not attractive," Felicity said ingenuously. "He's beautiful. It's the contrast between the two that intrigues me. One so pure, the other so delightfully decadent. But that doesn't mean I don't love Liam. I wouldn't be human if I didn't notice an attractive man when I see one. After all, I'm only eighteen."

"I believe that was at the core of your father's objections to Mr. Blackstone. It seems he was right."

"Oh, pooh!" Felicity scoffed. "Lord Marlowe was right. You are distressingly like Papa at times. Once I'm married to Liam I won't flirt with other men. If I could only overcome Liam's tiresome scruples! But as long as we're kept apart I have to keep my spirits up, don't I?"

"I would think you'd have an easier time convincing your father that you know your own mind if you didn't," Gillian observed. "And if I were you I wouldn't choose someone like Lord Marlowe as an object of your devotion. He's a bit more than you can handle."

"Gilly, how you misunderstand me!" Felicity laughed. "Lord

Marlowe is exactly the sort of person I *should* pick. He's got such a black reputation that Liam will seem like an absolutely brilliant match compared to him." She squeezed her aunt's numb hand. "I know what I'm doing. All I need work on now is Lord Marlowe. But I don't expect to have any trouble winding him around my little finger. There's never been a man I haven't been able to attach if I've wanted him," she added with simple pride.

"I wouldn't underestimate Lord Marlowe if I were you, Felicity," she said warningly. "He didn't seem too taken with you this afternoon."

"No, he seemed far more interested in you," Felicity agreed, obviously puzzled. "Perhaps he has better taste than one would have expected."

"*Merci du compliment.*" Gillian laughed. "I would abandon this scheme if I were you. You may bite off more than you can chew."

"But what a lovely mouthful," Felicity said wickedly, running up the broad front steps of the Redfern mansion before Gillian could reprove her.

# Chapter Five

IT *WAS* A LOVELY day for a stroll to Hookham's Lending Library, Gillian agreed innocently. Of course Felicity should take advantage of the unexpectedly clement weather. And would Felicity require her aunt to accompany her? Knowing her aunt's inordinate fondness for reading, that is. No? Felicity's somewhat flighty maidservant would be ample protection? But of course her aunt trusts her. Implicitly. She would have no doubts whatsoever of her obedient niece's occupation and destination for the next few hours. Oh, of course. The library.

Felicity breathed a sigh of relief once she was out of sight of the imposing edifice that was the Redfern mansion, and once out of range of Berkeley Square her spirits lightened still further. Obviously she hadn't fooled Gilly for a moment. She knew perfectly well where her wicked niece was heading, and Felicity didn't flatter herself that it was Gilly's faith in her that made her turn a blind eye to Felicity's transgressions. No, it was Gilly's wisely placed faith in the vicar's high principles that allowed her niece to keep a rendezvous with nothing more than a romantic maid in attendance.

Gillian must also have known, Felicity added ruefully, climbing into the hansom cab that Marjorie had deftly procured, just how romantic those little tête-à-têtes could be. They consisted of Felicity, her elegant gown covered by a capacious green stuff apron, dishing out loathsome bowls of steaming soup to the oddest assortment of people. Hollow-eyed mothers with ominously rosy cheeks that Liam told her bitterly signified consumption, cheery gentlemen well gone into the effects of what was popularly referred to as Blue Ruin, children young in years but ancient in the cruel way of the world. It was the children that distressed her tender heart the most. From the burned and starving chimney sweeps who'd grown too large for the chimneys and had been abandoned, the saucy pickpockets who treated her with a touching gallantry, to the angelic faces of those who sold their frail young bodies for the price of a meal. If she could, she would have bundled them all back to Berkeley Square with her. Gillian would have welcomed them with open arms. But she knew full well that was out of the question. Nevertheless, it wasn't only for the sake of Liam Blackstone's beautiful dark eyes that she ventured down into the most depraved section of the teeming city of London.

"I hope you're not expecting me to wait on those creatures," Marjorie sniffed as the carriage rattled over the uneven pavement. "And I wish there was some way I could talk you out of it. You could get fleas from the likes of them."

Felicity turned her attention from the slums outside the window and eyed her maid disapprovingly. "You will help me in whatever capacity Mr. Blackstone requires," she said in a cold tone of voice seldom used on her servant and confidant, "and you will do so with good grace. Jesus washed the feet of the sinner, you know."

Another disapproving sniff. "Why couldn't you fancy someone like young Mr. Blenkinthorp, who fair dotes on you? Or Sir Sidney Penstaff? Either one of those gentlemen would come up to scratch if you gave them the slightest bit of encouragement. But instead you moon around after a man who isn't even pleased to see you when you go to all the trouble to drag me down to this terrible place. I think you must have windmills in your head, Miss Felicity," she said with her usual frankness that refused to recognize a set-down.

Felicity didn't even bother to administer one this time. Her pulses were racing, her heart was pounding as the carriage drew up outside the shabby little mission that presently served as Liam Blackstone's parish house. "You sound like my father, Marjorie," she said shortly. "And if you don't mind your tongue and make an attempt to be more amenable, I'll take Gillian's Flossie with me next time. She'd be ripe for an adventure."

"You call this an adventure?" Marjorie demanded. "Slaving away for the worst kind of people? I doubt Flossie would find it so. And you know she can't keep a still tongue in her head."

"Neither can you. I know full well I have you to thank for my aunt's knowing where I go on the few afternoons we steal away. You are extremely lucky your interference didn't throw a rub in the way of my plans. Fortunately Aunt Gilly is the best of all my family, and enters into my feelings."

"I hadn't noticed that," Marjorie snapped. "I doubt she would have let you go if she hadn't known *I'd* be along to protect you."

"Fine protection you are. I expect Aunt Gillian knew perfectly well that a man of Liam's scruples wouldn't allow me to be compromised." If there was an aggrieved note in her voice as she contemplated how uncompromised she actually was, Marjorie had heard it all before.

"Are you going to sit here arguing all day, Miss Felicity?" she now inquired in a frosty tone. "Or are we to beard the lion in his den? Better still, are we to return home without venturing out of this nice, safe carriage?"

"There are times, Marjorie," Felicity remarked with deceptive sweetness, "when I wonder how you would like being relegated to the laundry back at Redfern Manor." With that dire threat she opened the door and swung out of the carriage, having learned to do so without her customary assistance on previous visits. Temporarily silenced by the threat, Marjorie followed her mistress.

The little mission overseen by the indefatigable Liam Blackstone was definitely unprepossessing on the outside. Unlike the mean little hovels that surrounded the aging brick building, it was a large, ungainly hovel, with a gloomy, dark-stained front and an inartistic sign proclaiming its services. That sign was the product of Mr. Blackstone, who had sharply spurned Miss Redfern's more artistic hand.

Inside the place was as appealing as rigorous cleanings could make it. There was not a speck of dirt in the large, barren meeting room that also served as a communal dining hall for the poor of the area, and a chapel when Mr. Blackstone could gather the proverbial two or more people together. The kitchen consisted of a large open fireplace on one wall, with a well-scrubbed chopping table and several large soup kettles that always seemed filled with a steaming concoction comprised of aging vegetables, the gifts of area merchants, and various arcane cuts of meat that Felicity suspected originated from exceedingly peculiar sections of exceedingly peculiar animals. Indeed, whenever she had managed to sneak a visit to Mr. Blackstone's mission, she was unable to eat anything but salt biscuits for twenty-four hours. But the poor, downtrodden unfortunates seemed glad enough for it, coming back to refill their cracked earthenware bowls as often as the long-suffering Marjorie would allow.

For once the great barren room was empty. A miserable fire was filling a small corner of the vast cavern with a great deal of smoke and less heat, and the long benches, white with scrubbing, were empty of their usual pitiful occupants. There was no strong scent of the redolent soup, and for this Felicity could only be grateful. Loosening the strings of her plainest bonnet, she ventured farther into the room, ignoring Marjorie's hissed protests.

"Where do you suppose everyone is?" she whispered, shivering slightly. "There was no sign on the front, was there? Surely Liam would have let me know if the mission was to be closed."

"I'm not so sure," Marjorie said grimly, and Felicity felt a momentary panic in her breast. A panic that was partially allayed when the door on the far side of the room opened, and Mr. Liam Blackstone, vicar of this small, poverty-stricken parish, stepped into the room.

It was not in any way surprising that Miss Felicity Redfern would have tumbled head over heels in love with Liam Blackstone, although it was a wonder that one of her heretofore flighty nature would have stayed constant in the face of such unpromising response. But constant she had stayed, and her pretty, heart-shaped face became radiant as she smiled upon her beloved. Liam Blackstone did not smile back, though his eyes brightened momentarily.

At the advanced age of twenty-six, Liam Blackstone was prematurely weighted down with the cares of the world. Born with a somewhat romantic disposition, leavened with a strong streak of spiritual leanings, a large dose of warmhearted compassion toward the poor, and an unfortunate streak of puritanism that threatened to smother him with feelings of acute worthlessness, Liam Blackstone was a somewhat confused young man. None of this, however, showed in his face.

If Lord Byron was considered a well-looking gentleman, Liam Blackstone put him entirely in the shade. He had a noble brow, adorned with jet black curls, a classical nose, perfectly molded lips, chiseled features, a pale golden complexion that was a healthy ruddy shade when he wasn't mortifying his flesh, high cheekbones, and the most melting dark eyes that had ever destroyed a young lady's peace of mind. That those melting dark eyes and his elegant lips at times attested to a sternly repressed but occasionally overwhelming sensual streak in his nature was no one's business but Liam Blackstone's and his tiresome conscience. And Felicity Redfern.

He moved into the room with his customary unconscious grace, glowering at his visitors, and Felicity found herself admiring his form in a far from spiritual manner. He was tall, but not too tall. Just the right height for her to rest her dark head on his shoulder. Those shoulders were broad, and if he was just a trace too thin at the moment, all he needed was a good woman to feed him. He was far too busy with the concerns of his desperate parish to pay much attention to his stomach, and when his normal appetite reminded him, he would ignore the cravings, determined that a truly spiritual man would not notice such mundane things. He had a great deal more success ignoring the clarion call of food than he had ignoring Miss Redfern's lithe presence.

"What are you doing here, Felicity?" he inquired in unwelcoming tones.

Felicity was daunted. She had seen the welcoming light in those sensuous dark eyes, and had seen it swiftly overlaid with disapproval. "I came to help, of course," she replied. "Marjorie and I thought we could give you some assistance."

"As you can see, no assistance is needed today. St. Barnabas's Parish is having a festival, and everyone is over there. Does your father know you are here?"

"My father pays no attention to his daughter's comings and goings," she replied innocently. "Goodness, he'd be bored to tears if I tried to keep him abreast of all the things that fill my time. I would think—"

"That is the problem, Felicity," Liam said sternly, moving toward her almost against his will. "You don't think the proper things. Your father has refused to consider my suit, and I must say I don't blame him. I can hardly provide for you in any way that would be the slightest bit comfortable. You are used to commanding the elegancies of life, and as the wife of a clergyman you would barely have enough to live on. I must always give freely to the poor, and you would be made to suffer for it. No new dresses, when there are people in rags about us, no seed cakes and ginger biscuits when children are starving."

"And do you think I'd care?" she cried, meeting him halfway in the middle of the room. "Don't you think you matter more to me than new dresses and seed cakes? I love you!"

"Don't!" There was a look of real pain on his beautiful face, and the pragmatic Marjorie gave a romantic sigh from her post by the door. "Your father has refused his consent, and that is that. I should have known better than to have listened to that wretchedly lustful part of my nature. When will I learn to school my passions?" he demanded of himself.

"Wretchedly lustful?" Felicity echoed in a hopeful tone. "But the only Christian outlet for lust is marriage, isn't it? Saint Paul said something about that, didn't he?"

"I am unworthy of you."

"Piffle!" she shot back, moving closer and looking up at him in a manner she was certain he could not resist. "It is you who are far too good for me, Liam. But with you to guide me I know I could improve. I would try very hard to be worthy of you."

He reached out his strong hands and grasped her upper arms, in an admonishing fashion, he told himself as his fingers caressed her soft flesh. "Felicity, it cannot be. You are too young to know your own mind."

"Stuff and nonsense! I've loved you for three years. Since I was fifteen years old and you were the curate in our village. And well you know it, no matter how you try to deny it. We waited until I was eighteen, and still my father was blind, stubborn, pigheaded, and cruel," she shot back. "Why must we argue about this every time, Liam? I understand that we cannot elope, and even if you won't admit it, I know you love me just as much as I love you. If you could only hold out some hope I could manage to bear it until I'm twenty-one. I understand that we can't run away to Gretna Green, but even three years would fly by if I knew I could be yours at the end of it."

"I cannot ask it of you!" he cried, the hands moving up her arms and drawing her closer.

"Oh, please, please ask it of me," she cried, tears of desperation in her fine dark eyes. "I would do anything for you, Liam. I want to be by your side, in the slums, in Canterbury, wherever you choose to go. You cannot shut me out."

"I can and I must." He held her body inches away from his own, so that he could feel the heat and smell her soft, flowery scent. With a groan he thrust her away.

She stared up at him with tragic eyes. "I don't believe you," she said. "What can I do to prove to you that I love you?"

His sensual mouth set in a thin line. "You can leave me alone."

There was a dead silence in the room, and even the fascinated Marjorie stopped breathing for a moment. "Do you mean that?"

"Yes," the very Christian gentleman lied.

"Does that mean I cannot come here and aid the poor?" Her voice was tight with pain and unshed tears.

"I cannot stop you. But I must deplore your sneaking out of the house with no one knowing—"

"My aunt knows where I am," she interrupted, her head held high. "Very well, Liam. I suppose I have no choice but to abide by your decision."

The capitulation was a bit too hasty for Mr. Blackstone, but he told himself he must be glad she had seen the light. "Can't you see, Felicity," he found himself saying, "that an alliance with me would only ruin you?"

"And can't you see, Liam," she replied in a cold, hurt voice, "that you are saving me for a life devoted to fashion and frivolity? I can only hope you do not regret your decision. There are a great many things worse than marrying an impoverished vicar." There was a note in her voice that filled Marjorie with the liveliest dread, having known her mistress for all of her eighteen rambunctious years.

Mr. Blackstone was similarly alarmed. "You would not do anything foolish?"

Felicity smiled brightly. "What else has a young lady to do with her time?" she inquired. "Besides spend it foolishly. I hope you enjoy your celibacy, Mr. Blackstone." And she swept from the mission with a shocked Marjorie at her heels, leaving Mr. Blackstone staring after her with a lovelorn expression and feeling of despair that wasn't the slightest bit leavened by the knowledge that he had acted for the best.

# Chapter Six

THE HONORABLE Bertram Talmadge, Gillian's oldest nephew, sat surveying the fire in the smaller drawing room at Berkeley Square, chin in hand, brown locks arranged a la Brutus, his clothing just bordering on the dandy, with an expression of deepest gloom on his handsome young features that he rather fancied resembled Byron's soulful torments, but in actuality resembled nothing so much as an advanced case of sulks. His sympathetic aunt was tactless enough to tell him so.

"I am not sulking, Gillian," he shot back, deeply offended. "But sometimes a man's got things on his mind. Nothing to bother the weaker sex with, of course. But we all have our burdens." He let out a noble sigh.

"Yes, dear. Are you sulking because you weren't invited to the Cherringtons' with your aunt and uncle? I assure you that you wouldn't want to go. Even Felicity is relieved to be excluded from the evening's torments. Watered punch and stale cakes do not number among my especial delights."

"As if I cared for such trumpery things," Bertram scoffed. "I've a great deal more on my mind than parties and such."

Gillian surveyed him with tolerant affection. The first of a seemingly endless line of nieces and nephews, he now, at the advanced age of nineteen, considered himself a gentleman of town bronze. Gillian suspected he fell far short of the mark and had noticed his increasing abstraction over the past two weeks since he had been sent down in disgrace from Oxford. A tentative question here and there was always turned off with a hearty laugh, but the haunted look had stayed in his trusting brown eyes, and he had developed a tendency to bite his full lower lip when no one was looking. "And what is on your mind, dearest?" she questioned gently. "If there's any way I can help, you have only to let me know."

"As if I'd bother my favorite aunt with a few silly problems," he scoffed, brushing a speck of imaginary lint from his coat. "A fine sort I'd be."

"But what else are aunts for? Truly, Bertie, I've been around for a bit and am not a complete innocent. You won't shock me, you know."

"Doing it rather too brown, Gilly. You're only eleven years older than I am, more like an older sister than an aunt. And one doesn't tell one's older sister everything." He jumped out of the comfortable seat and began pacing restlessly about the room. "I just need a bit of time, and everything will come round right in the end."

"Is it money, Bertie? Because if it is, I have a great deal, you know, and scarcely any use for it. You could have any amount . . ."

"I'd rather drown," he said fiercely. "I appreciate the thought, Gilly, but I know in my bones that the luck will change. It can't stay against me forever."

These artless confidences instilled even greater dread in Gillian's heart, and she was searching for a way to continue the discussion when Felicity floated into the room, a vision in pale pink muslin.

"Well, my aging aunt, you look positively terrible," she announced with her usual forthrightness. "Are you never going to wear your new green dress instead of that wretched gray thing? One would think you were in mourning."

"I am, darling," she replied flippantly. "For my lost youth."

An expression of absolute horror came over Felicity's delicate countenance. "Your lost youth!" she echoed, aghast. "Oh, my heavens, it cannot be March twenty-sixth already!"

Now it was Gillian's turn to blush. "I hadn't meant to mention it," she said apologetically. "It is extremely embarrassing for people when they forget."

"Forget what?" Bertie questioned, mystified.

"Today is Gillian's thirtieth birthday," Felicity declaimed in tragic tones. "And no one remembered."

"Why didn't you remind us?" accused Bertie. "How do you expect us to remember things like that when the world's in the state it's in?"

"Well, actually, I did mention it," Gillian ventured in a meek voice. "I said something about it last Friday, and then after church, and yesterday at breakfast." She smiled mischievously. "You see, I wanted to be certain I received a great many presents, but obviously I was served by my just desserts."

"Well, I'm not as wicked as I seem, Gilly," Felicity said, tossing herself down by her aunt with her customary lack of decorum. "I did try to buy you a present. You remember that pretty locket we saw in the jeweler's shop when Lord Marlowe walked us home? And the diamond ear-bobs you admired?"

"Felicity, dearest, they were both far too expensive!" Gillian protested.

"Well, I expected Papa would pay for them," she admitted with disarming honesty. "But they were both gone when I went back there the next day. And knowing how disparate our tastes are, I didn't dare choose something else for fear you'd hate it and feel you had to wear it all the time to please me. I did think of ordering the dress from Madame Racette's, but that would have been too expensive, and Papa would have had apoplexy."

"Darling, the thought is worth far more than the present." She embraced her niece's slender shoulders, laughing. "I would have had no place to wear such an indecent dress, apart from my bedroom, and though the locket or the earbobs would have been divine, I didn't really need them."

"A woman always needs more jewels," Felicity said. "To ensure her femininity."

"And where did you hear that?" Gillian demanded, fascinated.

"From Grandmama Smith-Davies, of course. Who else would I know who would look and talk like a courtesan?" questioned the young lady demurely.

"Well, I am in no great need of jewels to ensure *my* femininity," Gillian said in repressive tones belied by the sparkle in her eyes.

"I think it completely rotten that no one thought to celebrate your birthday."

"I am just as happy to celebrate it with my niece and nephew," Gillian replied.

"Very well, then we'll celebrate it. Bertie, go upstairs and put on full evening dress. Gilly, I want that nile green dress on you or I'll dress you myself. I'll send Marjorie in to do your hair—she's much better than your Flossie, you know. And I'll have Reynolds put champagne on ice, and Cook will make us up some festive little cakes . . ."

"Felicity, it's half past eight already," Gillian protested, laughing, as she was pushed from the room with Bertie.

"You see," Felicity said triumphantly. "It's quite early. The gaming salons don't open until ten, do they, Bertie?" There was hidden meaning in her voice, and Bertie turned a guilty red as he escorted Gillian toward her bedroom. In the distance they could hear Felicity's voice raised, giving excited orders to the servants.

"We might as well do what she says, Gillian," Bertie said with an effort at good cheer. "And don't worry, I'll go out and get you a present tomorrow. Can't think what made it slip my mind."

"Perhaps it was gaming debts, Bertie?" Gillian asked gently.

Bertie's face flamed. "Never you mind about them. They're not half as bad as most people I know. By the way, I didn't hear Felicity aright, did I? She couldn't have said Lord Marlowe walked you home, could she?"

"She could, and he did. He's a gentleman with a great deal of address. Have you met him?"

"A . . . a few times. I wouldn't have thought Uncle Derwent would approve of that."

"I'm sure he wouldn't," Gillian tossed it off lightly. "But then, there's a very great deal that Derwent doesn't approve of, and if one spent all one's time paying attention to it, one would have time for nothing else."

"You didn't always used to feel that way," Bertie observed shrewdly. "For as long as I can remember you've done exactly what everyone else has wanted you to do, and paid no attention whatsoever to your own needs and desires. What in the world has made you finally decide to consider yourself for a change?"

She stared at him, nonplussed. "I suppose it is abominably selfish of me."

"Not at all," Bertie protested. "It's about time someone thought of you for a change. You've got my backing, Gilly. Any help you need, just let me know."

"Bless you, love." She kissed him. "I'll remember the offer. For now you would please me no end if you would hurry up and change. I want some champagne. After all, it's not every day I turn thirty."


GILLIAN STARED AT her reflection in the dressing table mirror in the gleam of candlelight. The nile green dress was as pretty as she knew it would be, clinging tightly to her small, well-formed breasts, exhibiting an attractive expanse of chest and shoulder. Marjorie had dressed the red-gold hair in loose waves around her delicate head, framing the pretty face and softening her features. Her blue eyes were large and shining, the lips tremulous, the cheeks too pale. With a touch of defiance Gillian reached into her bottom drawer and pulled out a hidden rouge pot. A bit of charcoal to her lashes wouldn't come amiss either, she decided suddenly, a wave of unaccustomed anger and frustration sweeping over her. Her life was passing her by. There were slight mauve shadows under her large, brilliant eyes that hadn't been there a couple of years ago, and she fancied she could recognize the beginnings of faint lines on her petal-soft skin. It wasn't fair, she thought. To spend one's life at the beck and call of others, to have reached the advanced age of thirty years old and never been kissed, never been held in a man's arms, never known a man's love. And never would, no matter how pretty she looked in the soft glow of the candlelight. No one would see her but Felicity and Bertie—it would all be a waste. It was enough to drive a girl to drink, she thought a little wildly. But then, she was scarcely a girl anymore. And hadn't minded, until tonight.

"Be honest, Gillian," she told herself firmly, her voice light and breathless in the empty bedroom. "You started minding two and a half weeks ago." Flipping open her jewelry box, she surveyed the sparse contents.

In the battle for her mother's jewelry her older sisters and sister-in-law had proved their usual assertive selves, and Gillian, with the barest minimum of social life, had acquiesced gracefully enough. But Felicity's Grandmama Smith-Davies was right—it did make one feel more feminine to be adorned with jewels. Disgusted with her own maudlin self-pity, Gillian turned her jewelry box upside down and proceeded to bedeck herself with every single diamond she owned. A wide diamond necklace that Letty had stigmatized as old-fashioned but actually possessed too short a neck to do it justice, three diamond bracelets with weak catches and ornate settings, one ring (the sisters had a weakness for rings and from Mama's twenty-seven diamond rings could only spare one rather small one for Gillian) and two diamond hair clips in the shape of swans. She owed their possession to the fortunate instance of everyone else in the family having shorter hair.

The earbobs would have suited her to perfection, she thought, surveying her glittering reflection with a wry smile. Better to go without than to mar the glittering perfection of her toilette. At least, she thought defiantly, she was the prettiest thirty-year-old spinster she had ever seen. Not a complete antidote yet.

As a finishing touch she reached out for the scarcely used bottle of scent, a Christmas present from the same Grandmama Smith-Davies. It was a deep, subtle fragrance that Derwent had stigmatized as tawdry. Well, tonight she felt tawdry, and mysterious, and blatantly sensual. She splashed it liberally around her neck and shoulders and in the vee between her breasts, dusted a touch more rouge on her high cheekbones, and sailed from the room, a satisfied smile on her lips.

"Good heavens, Gillian, is that you?" Felicity demanded. "You look positively ravishing, doesn't she, Bertie?"

"Positively!" he agreed, somewhat dazed at his aunt's transformation. Remembering his duties, he handed his aunt a large, bubbling glass of iced champagne. "You said you wanted some right away."

"Indeed I do." She took a small sip, sighed, and drained the glass, holding it out for more. "I intend to drink a very great deal of champagne tonight, and eat those lovely little cakes I see, and be extremely gay. Thank you, Bertie." She started in on her second glass.

"Are you certain you ought to, Gilly?" Felicity asked. "You aren't used to spirits, and I shudder to think what Papa would say if he were to return home and find us all above ourselves."

"I would say it would serve him right, to forget Gillian's birthday," Bertie averred, having imbibed a bit freely already. "And I think we should dashed well celebrate Gillian's birthday any way she pleases. And if she pleases that we all drink a great deal of champagne, then I'm with her."

"Done!" cried Felicity, draining her glass with relish. "Just don't tell poor Liam what depths I've sunk to."

"No one's likely to see him except you, idiot!" said her cousin amiably. "Though why you want to get leg-shackled to such a dashed dull stick is beyond my comprehension. Anyone who would accept Uncle Derwent's decree without making any effort to fight it seems pretty milk pudding to me." He poured himself and the two ladies more champagne, spilling the wine somewhat.

"He's not a dull stick!" Felicity defended her true love. "He simply has very high principles, something you're completely unacquainted with."

"Very amusing. I wonder you can find any man to marry you with a tongue like yours. More champagne, Gilly?" He poured before she could agree, and she cheerfully downed her fourth glass.

"I do wish you wouldn't argue on my birthday," she said plaintively, moving with unsteady grace to the sofa by the banked fire. "I truly hate it. Why can't everything be pleasant all the time?" she inquired soulfully, stifling a delicate little hiccup.

"Because life ain't like that," Bertie said bluntly, striking his Byronesque pose.

"Oh, cut line, Bertie," Felicity snapped. "You do get tremendously tiresome at times."

"Well, then, it's a great deal fortunate that I have no intention of marrying you," he shot back, affronted.

"Marrying me?" she scoffed, tossing her head. "That's a rare jest."

"Not if our parents have their way," Bertie said gloomily. "Your father's been dropping all sorts of hints since I've come to stay, and my parents have been after me since Christmas."

Shock made Felicity sink to the sofa beside her aunt. "How simply ghastly. I had no idea."

Bertie sat down beside the two of them, sunk in companionable gloom. "Thought you didn't. But you know what our parents are like when they've got a maggot in their brains. I've been counting on Gilly to keep 'em in line, but I'm not sure that she can hold out much longer."

Felicity turned her great blue eyes toward her aunt. "Do you think they can make us? We should make a horrid pair, you know. Besides, I love Liam."

"And I have no intention of getting married for a good long time," Bertie added.

"They may very well try," Gillian conceded, swirling the dregs of her champagne and slopping just a tiny bit on her green silk skirt. "But I have little doubt you two are more than a match for them. If worse comes to worse you will simply have to elope with your vicar, Felicity."

"Gilly, you're drunk!"

"Heavens, no, child," she said sweetly, moving over to the table on skittering feet and pouring herself another glass. "Merely very happy. And right now I think every member of the illustrious Redfern family can go to the devil. Present company excepted, of course. I fail to see why you should sacrifice your happiness on the altar of family duty. One is enough." She raised her glass. "Cheers."

"Oh, Gilly, do you feel you've been sacrificed?" Felicity questioned with tearful and champagne-induced sympathy.

"What else are virgins for?" Gillian inquired with simplicity.

"I say, Gilly, you ought to watch your language." Bertie's shirt points seemed to have grown suddenly tighter. "You never know who might hear you."

"No one will hear me," she said sadly. "Look, even Felicity has gone to sleep."

Bertie looked at his cousin's sleeping form with disgust. "Can't hold her wine," he pronounced.

"Ah, but *I* can, dearest Bertie," Gillian announced. "And I think we must be careful not to wake her up. We should leave."

"Leave?" Bertie echoed.

"Absolutely. All this finery shouldn't be wasted on a nephew.

Where can we go?"

"I have no idea," he said uneasily, sobering a bit.

"Where did Derwent and Letty go? We could follow them."

"Good God, no! We weren't invited."

"I wouldn't think that would matter on my birthday," she said soulfully.

"Well, I wouldn't think so either, but you never can tell. We might go to the opera," he suggested rather wildly.

She shook her head. "Too late. It's almost eleven. Now where can we possibly go where it won't be too late for . . . Bertie!"

Her nephew jumped guiltily. "I think we should stay home."

"I know where we can go. Gaming salons are just beginning to be lively right about now, aren't they? And I have a great deal of money. We shall go and gamble. I am bound to be in luck on my birthday."

"I don't think that would be a good idea," Bertie said weakly.

"And I know exactly where we should go. Lord Marlowe's establishment. I'm certain he'll be delighted to see us."

Bertie's complexion was an alarming combination of pale horror and rosy embarrassment, with a touch of green around the gills. "I don't know where it is."

"Now don't prevaricate, Bertie. You were the one who told Felicity about it. You needn't worry—Lord Marlowe and I are old friends. He's scarcely likely to turn us away from the door. Is he?"

"He doesn't turn anyone of good ton from the door. And some of bad ton are just as welcome. Though I sometimes think that's more Vivian Peacock's doing," he added darkly.

"And women are allowed?"

"With someone like Marlowe?" Bertie scoffed. "Women are encouraged. But not your sort of woman, Gilly."

"Lightskirts?" she questioned knowledgeably, handing a fresh bottle of champagne to Bertie to open.

"Nooo. But ladies who are not really top-drawer. There's Lady Kempton, of course, and Sally Jersey can be seen there any number of evenings. Of course, she always had a weak spot for a handsome man, no matter what his reputation."

"Well, that settles it. If a patroness of Almack's may go there with impunity, then a Redfern need not blush to be seen there also. We'll finish this bottle, Bertie, and then be off. Cheers!"

# Chapter Seven

THE WEEKS SINCE Ronan Patrick Blakely, Lord Marlowe, the marquis of Herrington, had returned to his native shores had been busy ones. His lordship had been greatly amused to discover that what was completely unacceptable in an impoverished younger son was lauded as being delightfully original in a wealthy marquis. Even young Ronan Blakely's final escapade, which involved attempting to elope with a married woman of impeccable lineage, was now looked upon twenty years later as an amusing prank.

One of the strangest aspects of his re-entry into society was the attitude of mothers. The gentlemen accepted him, which was only to be expected. Marlowe was a man's man, with easy, charming manners around his peers that had always made him universally well liked, despite his predilection for the petticoat line. But unlike his youth, when the mothers of husband-hunting daughters would refuse to allow their precious offspring to stand up with such a rake, nowadays he was considered an extremely eligible parti. How often, one matron with a gangly, bracket-faced daughter demanded of another with an equally unfortunate child, does a handsome, wealthy, *titled* gentleman of excellent lineage come along? What had put him beyond the pale before were now dismissed as youthful peccadilloes; what had caused mothers to snub him outright were now treated as entertaining eccentricities.

It was little wonder that a man of Marlowe's cynical nature would endeavor to discover just how far his pardon extended. Would the proper Miss Chansforth care for a stroll in the deserted garden? Miss Chansforth would be delighted. But wouldn't her mother mind? Oh, no, Mama told her that Lord Marlowe was to be deferred to in all matters. Whatever would give him pleasure. Whatever, Miss Chansforth?

Such sport soon paled for Marlowe. For one thing, the majority of the ladies, though extremely pretty, were idiots, with nothing to say for themselves. Strumpets, out to sell their bodies to the highest bidder who came complete with wedding license, yet lacking the easygoing honesty of their less legal-minded sisters. And besides, they were all so damnably *young.* By the time he met Gillian Redfern, women, that is, proper ladies, had been relegated to a very minor position in his scheme of things.

"You can't do that, old man," protested Vivian Peacock. "Got to get leg-shackled sometime. And you've been raising hopes in several breasts. They won't like it that you've lost interest."

"Well, I can't very well marry both Miss Chansforth and Miss Waterford," replied Marlowe amiably. "I think I'd best forget about the weaker sex altogether for now. They can be damnably disrupting."

"Does that include forgetting about Miss Redfern?" Vivian toyed idly with his brandy glass, an absorbed expression on his puffy face.

Marlowe cocked an eye at him. "We have a wager on, do we not? A gentleman never forgets a wager. Besides, I have the suspicion that Gillian Redfern is a great deal more interesting than these misses just out of the schoolroom. Have we set a time limit on that wager?"

"Not yet. How long do you think it would take you to bring her around? It wouldn't do to overestimate your powers," said Viv with just a hint of malice. "I want to win, but I want it to be fair. It's late March now—what do you say to the end of the season? Late May?"

"More than enough time."

"It may not be as easy as you think," Peacock cautioned.

"It may not be as difficult," retorted Marlowe. "She's already unwillingly fascinated by the first rake she's ever met in her sheltered life. Once I set my mind to it, it shouldn't take much time at all."

"You're forgetting that damnably starched-up family."

Marlowe dismissed them with an airy wave of his hand. "I expect them to prove more a help than a hindrance. Gillian Redfern is not going to like being ordered about by her cod's head of a brother."

"She has for her entire life. Why should she change?"

Marlowe smiled slowly. "I'm going to introduce her to a few things far more pleasurable. Derwent Redfern should pale in comparison."

Vivian eyed his friend warily. "Is this quite kind of us?" he inquired casually. "After all, you wouldn't want to step too far beyond the line of what is pleasing. If Sally Jersey were to hear of this she might consider it too much."

"Why, Viv, I never knew you had a conscience. After all, this was your idea," Marlowe said lazily. "And I wouldn't worry if I were you. I intend to see to it that Gillian Redfern's heart is bruised but not broken. When we part she'll be more than ready to fall in love with someone a great deal more eligible, and will never again take the easy way out by burying herself among her demanding family." He lit a cheroot with a practiced air and surveyed the smoke with a faint smile of satisfaction. "I consider this an errand of mercy."

"You would," Vivian scoffed.

BUT THERE HADN'T been much time for the furtherance of their schemes. The problem of finding a suitable residence for his gaming hell, decorating and outfitting and staffing it took up all his spare time. The thousands of decisions involved in setting up a gaming house proved to be quite overwhelming. There were servants to hire, including the French chef whose duty was to provide the elegant champagne suppers *de rigueur* for all gamesters. There were a thousand wax candles to order, and a thousand greasy tallow ones for the kitchens. There were invitations and bribes to be offered, and all manner of tedious detail to fill Marlowe's usually indolent days. The first of which was the proper piece of real estate.

"I still don't see why your own house wouldn't do," Vivian had protested as they chased around for a residence large enough, with a properly elegant location. "Blakely House would have been perfect."

"I realize you think I'm lost to every vestige of propriety, Viv," he'd replied easily, "but my ancestors would spin in their graves if I were to turn the old place into a den of iniquity. Not that I owe them that much, but I suppose there must be one or two situations where I can be traditional. Besides, were I to have a gaming hell in my own home, how could I ever escape from the noise and intrusion? There are times when I need my privacy. No, a largish house somewhere near St. James's Street will do very well. I'll have private apartments there, of course, but Blakely House must be kept separate."

"But, Ronan, have you considered the cost? You may have forgotten that I helped your cousin manage his affairs the last few years, and I am aware that he was none too plump in the pocket. He could hardly have left you enough for such a grandiose scheme. And frankly, dear boy, I don't think I could afford to invest that kind of capital. Things haven't been going that well on the 'Change recently. I know I promised I'd be a full partner, but I'm afraid if it involves buying a place I can't . . ."

"Vivian, your excellent advice will be more than enough contribution to our little enterprise," he soothed. "And although Cousin Beowulf didn't leave me much except the title, the houses, and a number of debts, my years abroad were not wasted. Vienna was remunerative, and my years in India were positively absurd. At this point I can live quite lavishly on income alone. So you see, you needn't worry. I'm afraid I'm a regular Golden Ball."

Nothing but surprised pleasure showed in Vivian's dissipated countenance. "How splendid, Ronan! I had no idea you were so full of juice. In that case, I happened to hear of a cozy little house just off St. James's that could be turned into something quite special, provided there's a small outlay of cash to put it in order. I could arrange for us to see it tomorrow."

The house was duly seen, purchased, and the small outlay of cash required to turn it into a fashionable gaming hell began to reach staggering levels. Marlowe paid the bills without blinking, his mind on other things, his trust entirely on his old friend Vivian.

There was no way a gambling hell owned by society's newest and most outrageous darling could fail, although Vivian was doubtless gratified to find that it succeeded beyond his wildest expectations. Every night the place was an absolute crush, with baccarat, piquet, faro, dice, and even an e.o. table offered by the most elegant and charming of dealers. Marlowe would survey it all with his customary unruffled amusement, tiring of the entire thing before it even started. But it kept Vivian occupied, and provided a decent place to go for a hand or two of piquet when one was bored, as one too frequently was in the stultified London air. He wondered whether he ought to try the countryside.

The night of March twenty-sixth was some improvement. It was past eleven, with the evening's play just beginning to heat up, when there was a stunned lull in the conversation. Marlowe looked up from a hand of piquet to see Bertram Talmadge, a far too frequent *habitué* of these rooms, escort a very pretty lady in nile green into the room. The lady was staring about her in open fascination, and it was with a shock that Marlowe recognized Gillian Redfern.

# Chapter Eight

GILLIAN HAD NEVER before in her life stepped inside the wicked portals of a gaming hell, and she was busy experiencing a great deal of disappointment combined with a feeling of ill-usage. There was essentially no difference between the elegant, understated decor of the upper drawing room of 39 St. James's Street, where Marlowe's had its existence, and her sister Pamela's withdrawing room in Winchester. The same silk drapes, although Marlowe favored a dusky rose color, the same elegant, damask-covered furniture, the same genteel company and low murmur of voices. The only difference between Marlowe's upper room and the sort of card party one might find in the best homes in the city was the existence of the infamous e.o. table. And the fact that almost every guest there that night was male.

Gillian turned to her nephew, who fidgeted with his suddenly constricting collar and disrupted the folds of his Orientale cravat. "But where are the fallen women?" she inquired in what Bertie considered to be a damnably carrying voice.

"Please, Gilly!" he hushed her, his face turning beet red as he tried to avoid the curious gazes of his fellow gamesters. "The company here is very select. Guests are here by invitation only—not just your usual hugger-mugger are allowed in."

A look of consternation passed over her face. The champagne was beginning to fade a trifle, and old habits were struggling for possession. "Should we be here, then?" she inquired with a trace of anxiety.

"Of course," he reassured her, wishing heartily that he had thought of this excuse earlier. "*I* have the *entrée*, and am welcome to bring any guests I choose."

"I should have known. Bertie, have you gotten yourself into trouble here?" she questioned, her maternal instinct coming to the fore.

"Nothing I cannot get out of," he said stubbornly. "I wish you wouldn't worry so. I know what I'm—"

"Miss Redfern." Marlowe's smooth voice interrupted them, and Bertie turned a brighter red. "We are honored that you've condescended to visit our humble club." His tone was lazily insinuating, and Gillian turned to look up at him, the last bit of euphoria fleeing in sudden self-consciousness.

The jet-black evening clothes made him appear even taller in the candlelight, and the smile on his shadowed, handsome face was curiously disturbing. For the fifth time in the last three minutes, Gillian regretted her rash decision.

"Good evening, Lord Marlowe." None of this indecision and regret was in her cool, low voice. "I trust you don't mind that my nephew brought me along tonight. I wished to see what occupied such a great deal of his time." It was a shot in the dark, and Gillian could see by the deepening of Bertie's ruddy cheeks that it had hit the mark.

"Mr. Talmadge doesn't spend all his time here, Miss Redfern," Marlowe protested lightly. "I gather White's and Watier's share his patronage equally."

Worse and worse, thought Gillian, uncomfortably aware of the covert glances cast in her direction by the seemingly absorbed gamblers around her. There was Derwent's close friend Pinkthorp staring at her unabashedly before he bent to whisper something to the red-faced gentleman opposite him. They both laughed, and Gillian squirmed uneasily. There must be some way to extricate herself and her card-besotted nephew with both grace and dispatch, but her still somewhat fuzzy brain couldn't comprehend what it might be.

"Do you go along and join Peacock," Marlowe directed the hapless Bertie with a casual dismissal. "I will see to Miss Redfern's entertainment."

Bertie looked suitably torn. "But I promised my aunt . . ." he began weakly.

"Your aunt will be safe with me, Talmadge," said Marlowe, and there was nothing Bertie could do but bow himself away, his youthful face a study of misery and frustration.

"Poor Bertie," Gillian sighed.

"Poor Gillian," Marlowe corrected. "You're far too young to be that scamp's aunt. And you certainly shouldn't have the care of him adding to your other burdens."

She met his gaze coolly, only briefly disconcerted by the gleam in those dark green eyes. "I'm afraid you have it somewhat turned around, my lord. It is I who am his burden."

"Not tonight," he replied, drawing her arm through his and leading her past the hidden glances of his curious guests. "I was wondering how I could persuade you to grace my establishment. I have been on the lookout for you any number of occasions these past weeks, but you don't seem to go out in society much. To what do I owe the honor of your visit tonight?"

Disbelief warred with delight within her at the thought of Marlowe looking for her. Disbelief won. She ignored both emotions stoically. "I am celebrating attaining my majority," she replied solemnly, accepting the glass of champagne he handed her with the erroneous conclusion that one more wouldn't do much damage.

"You have reached the advanced age of twenty-one?" he inquired, sipping at his own glass while his eyes kept hers captive.

Gillian, in her lamentable fashion so recently acquired, drained the glass. "Thirty," she replied succinctly.

Marlowe's smile was gently mocking. "Such a very great age, to be sure," he murmured. "I don't know that I should be seen in public talking with such an aged hag. I have my reputation to consider."

"It's all very well for you to jest," she replied, as he refilled her glass. "But I have lines!"

He peered closely, and she could feel his warm breath on her skin. "Your head is full of windmills," he replied frankly. "I cannot see a single line, and furthermore it would only add character to a face that is far too pretty."

Needless to say, Gillian found this extremely pleasing. "At least," she said, "I can now be comfortable. No one will look twice at a lady of my advanced age when she ventures out unaccompanied. What would be frowned upon in a young ingenue cannot be thought singular in a woman of my years."

"Much as I regret disillusioning you, I am afraid I must. You have been the cynosure of every eye since you set foot inside this room. A great deal can be laid to the fact that you are in extremely elegant looks tonight, but part of it must be ascribed to the fact that very few properly brought up and behaved young ladies set foot inside a gaming hell, no matter how exclusive. And when that proper young lady is none other than Derwent Redfern's sister, and has heretofore been odiously starched-up herself, it's no wonder they are all staring at you."

"I am not odiously starched-up!" she shot back, stung.

"You were well on your way to being so when I happened along," he replied, unmoved. "And I would think we might be a great deal more comfortable in my private rooms in the back. I can promise you a late supper far above the general run of things, and a hand of piquet that should quite shatter you. Besides, I have something for you."

She stared up at him, suspicion warring with the lulling effects of the wine and his dark green eyes. "I wouldn't think it would be at all the thing for me to be closeted in your rooms, sir."

"I like the snippy way you call me 'sir,'" he said disconcertingly. "And I thought we had decided that your advanced age rendered you immune from criticism. Surely no one would suspect such an antidote capable of lascivious behavior?"

He was quizzing her, and she longed to give him the sharp set-down he so richly deserved, but the words and the real desire to do so escaped her. Sighing, she nodded, letting him lead her past the now scandalized eyes of the gamblers with a trepidation she told herself was patently absurd.

The moment she stepped into the private compartment at the back of the house all her doubts assailed her anew, and she took an instinctive step backward, directly into Lord Marlowe's solid form. Jumping away nervously, she watched him close the heavy panelled door behind them with absurd misgivings. He caught her somewhat desperate expression and smiled suddenly.

"You don't like my rooms?" he asked softly. "I consider them quite comfortable. I had them decorated with just such occasions in mind."

It seemed to Gillian's melodramatic mind that the smile that had so enchanted her was suddenly very sinister, and she wondered if anyone would hear her if she were to scream for help. "What sort of occasions?" she managed to choke out.

The smile broadened. "Why, dinner and a partie or two of cards with a friend," he replied smoothly. "Unless you had something else in mind?"

Gillian felt color suffuse her skin, and once more cursed her ready blushes. Before she could reply, however, he took her gloved hand and led her across the Aubusson-carpeted room to a rose velvet sofa, depositing her there but making no effort to join her. She breathed a small sigh of relief, allowed herself to relax just a tiny bit, and once more surveyed her surroundings.

It had been the sight of the bed that had panicked her, she realized. Mind you, it was at the very end of the room, shrouded discreetly in heavy gold curtains, and a lady wouldn't have even noticed its presence in an otherwise charming apartment. But Gillian was never one to be able to control unruly thoughts, and her attention kept slipping to that far end of the room, much to Marlowe's obvious amusement.

"I spend the night here on occasion," he explained, and Gillian blushed more deeply, then stared up at him defiantly.

"A gentleman would not have mentioned such a thing," she said repressively.

"But I am no gentleman, Gillian. I am a hardened rake, or had you forgotten? And why shouldn't I mention it, when you are so obviously fascinated by its presence? If I hadn't been directly behind you, I don't doubt you would have fled the room the moment you saw it. And then what would my curious guests have said? I shudder to think on it." He took a chair not too distant from her sofa, and stretched his long, elegant legs out in front of him. "In point of fact I stay here all night long on a great many occasions, and it is far too tedious to have to struggle across town to Blakely House when I am in need of a few hours' rest. The bed is there for that purpose, and not to seduce nervous little virgins."

The word shocked her even more than the bed had, but the shock had a salubrious effect that Marlowe had no doubt anticipated. She sat bolt upright, her eyes shining, shoulders back, tremulous mouth set in a brave smile. "I should think not," she agreed. "You could certainly do a great deal better than me if you set your mind to it."

"Now you are fishing for compliments, Gillian," he reproved gently. "And I make it a habit never to compliment a lady who stands so little in need of it. What do you fancy for supper? My chef has an especially delightful way with lobster that is much admired. Or if you prefer sweets, I brought my pastry chef from Vienna when I was called home to my coronet and duty."

"I . . . I'm not really hungry."

"With the amount of champagne you have already drunk it would behoove you to try to sop it up with a bit of food," he observed. "I have no desire to have you pass out on me in the midst of a hand of piquet." He rose with his lazy grace and pulled the bell cord. "I am persuaded once a meal is set before you you'll discover an appetite. Young Talmadge is doubtless deep in play by now, and he is unlikely to remember your existence for hours. We might as well beguile the time as best we can on your birthday. Which reminds me, I believe I said I had something for you." He rose and moved to the far end of the room, leaving Gillian to sit there, doubts creeping back, wondering whether she dared try to find Bertie amongst those so-curious guests of Marlowe's, or whether she should simply try to discover for herself a back stairway. A carriage shouldn't be too difficult to find, she imagined. In any case, Berkeley Square was not too terribly distant. She had walked farther many times in the country. Although there might be a slight difference between strolling accompanied in broad daylight through rolling green fields and sneaking along the deserted London streets at an hour much advanced. She was still pondering her best course when Marlowe turned back, and his tall, saturnine figure effectively banished all such thoughts. As long as she was in his presence and still lamentably in alt, she would go nowhere.

He placed a small velvet box in her hand, then took the seat opposite her, still declining the capacious sofa. "Go ahead, Gillian. I have held it for weeks, waiting for the proper moment to present it to you. I would think your thirtieth birthday would be eminently suitable."

With fumbling fingers she opened the box. The diamond earbobs she had so admired lay nestled on a bed of green velvet. Gillian closed the box and her eyes in dismay. "I cannot accept these," she murmured helplessly.

"My dear Gilly," Marlowe said in that caressing voice as he took the box out of her nerveless fingers, "you have no choice in the matter. Haven't you discovered by now that I do not take no for an answer?" When she opened her eyes she found he was deftly removing the earbobs from the box. Before she could guess his intent, he had caught her chin in one strong hand and was proceeding to put the earrings on for her. "Don't jerk about," he ordered briskly. "I wouldn't want to hurt your ear. But I *will* have my way."

There was nothing Gillian could do but sit there and allow him to place the earrings in her ears. The intimacy of the gesture had her beyond blushing, and only the knowledge that a great deal of experience with other women's bodies enabled him to carry out the mission with such deft dispatch kept her from refining too much upon it.

"I suppose I have no choice but to thank you, sir," she said in a muffled tone as he stepped back to admire his handiwork.

"No choice at all," he agreed, smiling down at her with that reckless, endearing smile that crinkled the corners of his eyes and forced an answering smile from her wary mouth.

"And now, before supper arrives, we must toast your birthday," he continued, handing her another glass of the seemingly endless supply of champagne that had flowed that night. "It is not every day that a young lady attains her majority. I am certain the diamond earbobs are paltry compared to your other gifts, but I find them particularly suited to you."

She took another sip from her champagne, another step down the road to perdition. "Hardly paltry, sir. Not only are they the only unsuitable gift I have ever accepted from a gentleman not a member of my own family, they are, in truth, the only gift I have received at all today."

A quick frown knit his brow. "Do you mean to tell me that no one remembered your birthday?"

"I can scarcely blame them," she replied with a rueful smile. "After all, I have had so *very* many."

"Gilly . . ." he began suddenly, when a loud knocking interrupted them. "Go away," he ordered crossly, but the heavy door opened anyway, filling Gillian with a relief that it hadn't been locked. A relief that quickly vanished as she recognized Bertie's panicked face.

"Excuse me," he mumbled, embarrassment and terror overwhelming him. "But Uncle Derwent's here! Felicity must have let something slip. He demands to know where you are. I've denied everything, but he intends to make a thorough search!"

"Not of my house, he doesn't," Marlowe stated in a cold, implacable voice.

"Don't be absurd," Gillian said, rising slowly, her heart pounding in a fear she told herself was absurd and unnatural. "Tell Derwent to wait for me below. I will join him in a moment."

"Good gracious, Gilly, you don't mean to admit that you're here!" Bertie gasped.

"I can't see what else I can do. Any number of people saw me come in here tonight and will doubtless be happy to tell him so. I don't wish to have Derwent make a cake of himself more than he already has, and I certainly don't wish him to insult Lord Marlowe further."

"But he'll be furious, Gilly."

Gillian took a deep breath. "Derwent is only human, Bertie. You have to know how to manage him. Go and tell him I'll be along immediately."

Bertie withdrew, shaking his head ominously. Putting her empty glass down on the table, she smiled very prettily up at Marlowe, hoping the trepidation wouldn't show in her fine blue eyes. It was a vain hope.

"Should I go with you?" he questioned abruptly. "Or would I only make things worse?"

"Definitely the latter. As soon as I get him home I'll be able to explain, but I dislike above all things the thought of a public brangle. Derwent is odiously difficult on occasion."

"Stiff-rumped I believe was the term," Marlowe said nonchalantly, reaching out a strong hand and placing it on her arm. "This is hardly a proper way to celebrate your majority. We shall have to plan it better next time."

"Next time?"

"You promised to have dinner and cards with me." His hand tightened slowly on her arm.

"Well, perhaps . . ."

"Unless you are frightened of your brother's disapproval?" he taunted.

"Don't be absurd. Derwent doesn't run my life."

"I'm glad to hear it. Besides not accepting unsuitable gifts from gentlemen who are not members of your family, what else have you failed to do in your thirty long years?" he inquired. "Have you ever been kissed? That is, by a gentleman who is not a member of your family?"

"I'll have you know I once fancied myself very much in love. Back when I was a green girl. And he loved me!" she said defiantly.

A small smile quirked the corners of his mouth. "But did he ever kiss you?"

She looked up, startled to find herself suddenly so close to him. "Of course not! He had too much respect for me."

"What a slow-top. It is fortunate I am so lacking in respect," he said, drawing her unresisting body into his arms, "because it is clearly past time." His mouth descended on hers with a thoroughness that left in no doubt that he considered she had indeed reached her majority. She could hear his heart beating through the clothing that separated them, feel his arms about her in a way that was positively possessive, as his hot mouth came down on hers. It seemed to brand and search her, and she knew she should fight, scream, or faint, that some resistance was definitely called for. She decided she could always blame the champagne, and entwined her arms about his neck, answering his mouth to the best of her limited experience.

That devastating kiss seemed to go on forever, and yet was far too short. He pulled back, looking down at her with a tender, mocking smile. "Not bad for a first attempt," he said huskily, and bent his head again.

Finally sense took hold of Gillian's addled brain. Wrenching herself from the warm comfort of his arms, she ran from the room as if the very devil were after her. Marlowe watched her graceful figure vanish with a troubled expression in his dark green eyes. Leaning down, he picked up her discarded champagne glass, held it aloft in a silent toast, and drained it.

# Chapter Nine

IT WAS SCARCELY the most pleasant ride home that evening. Not a word issued forth from Derwent Redfern's glowering face, though the heavy jowls were set in deep disapproval, the flinty eyes promising a ghastly retribution once they had attained the fastness of Redfern House. Bertie trailed along, head down, suitably abashed. Gillian had little doubt he had already sustained a severe tongue lashing, and she wondered how long Derwent could restrain himself. As they jolted along the rutted London streets in the darkness, Gillian allowed herself a small smile. Her lips were still burning from Marlowe's kiss, and she decided quite frankly that the embrace had been an even more delightful present than the earbobs swinging from her delicate ears. So that was what real kissing was like. How deliciously wonderful! Never again, of course, but at least now she understood what all the fuss was about, why girls longed to get married. Yet somehow she couldn't imagine any man but Marlowe could kiss with such devastating effect.

She stared across the darkened interior of the carriage at her brother's set face, and wondered idly why she wasn't in more of a panic. It usually required only a mild frown from Derwent's heavy face to set her in a taking. But not tonight. She had reached her majority, been kissed by one of the most attractive men she had ever met, and she wasn't about to let her overbearing brother's megrims spoil it for her. And she would tell him so, once he broached the subject. As a matter of fact, she was, for the first time in her life, quite looking forward to a good dust-up. Stripping off the thin kid gloves, she surreptitiously brushed her fingers along her tremulous lips. Lips that Marlowe had found worthy of kissing, she reminded herself, and her eyes were shining.

She realized with a start of surprise that the carriage had come to a halt outside Redfern House. "You will have no trouble seeing yourself off to bed, Bertram," Derwent was saying in his lugubrious voice. "My sister and I wish to be private."

"Of course, Uncle," Bertie said cravenly as he jumped down from the carriage. Derwent made no move to follow him. "Aren't you coming in?" he stammered nervously.

"In my own good time," his uncle replied. "What I have to say to your aunt doesn't want overhearing by a bunch of servants with nothing more constructive to fill their time than listening to their betters."

Always agile, Gillian scrambled from the carriage just ahead of Derwent's admonishing grip. "Well, I don't care to be cloistered in a carriage with you, Derwent," she said boldly, and Derwent's heavy eyebrows went up. "It's cold and I'm tired. If you have anything to say to me you may come into the drawing room and do so. Otherwise you may sit in this carriage till judgment day. Bertie, your arm." She swept up the front steps, her hand firmly on Bertie's weak and trembling arm.

"Gilly, how could you dare?" he breathed, tripping over the top step. "Uncle Derwent was already in a rare taking. He'll be livid after this."

"I doubt he could be any angrier," she replied as she stepped into the warm front hall and handed her pelisse to the impassive butler. "Derwent always was a bully, even as a child. It amazes me that I had forgotten," she mused. "He's bound to give me a dressing down and sulk for a few days. Or even threaten to pack me off to your parents or Pamela. But in the end Letty's comfort will come first, and you know she cannot manage her children without me around."

Bertie looked astounded at his aunt's plain speaking. "I never knew you to be so cynical, Gilly."

"I'm not cynical. Merely realistic. At the advanced age of thirty I am surely past romantic idealism."

"I don't know that Lord Marlowe would agree with that," Bertie offered, and then clammed up as Derwent stomped into the hallway, his face thunderous.

"Go to bed, Bertram," he snapped. "Unless you prefer to return to your parents tomorrow morning."

Bertie, bless his heart, looked torn, Gillian observed with amusement—torn between abject terror of her bullying brother and a desire to defend his hapless aunt. Terror won, and with mumbled apologies he disappeared up the stairs, leaving her to face the bearlike presence in front of her.

"Would you deign to attend me in my study?" he inquired with awful sarcasm, "or would that be too much to request?"

A shiver of nervousness washed over her, and she set her mind firmly on a certain rakish gentleman, squaring her shoulders and meeting her brother's glare with an amiable smile. "Certainly, brother," she replied calmly. "Though I don't see why you can't say what you want to me now and have done with it. The servants are just as likely to overhear us there as right here in the hallway."

Derwent hesitated, frustration turning his heavy features a mottled red. But still Gillian made no move toward the study, and drawing a deep, disapproving breath, he plunged into his diatribe. "Gillian, I am most disturbed! How could you have gone to such a place, with that young idiot as your only attendant? Don't you realize what sort of reputation Lord Marlowe enjoys? And how very singular you must appear to have gone to his gaming hell? I don't know what Sir Eustace Pogrebin will have to say to all this when he hears of it."

"What has Sir Eustace Pogrebin to say to anything?" Gillian demanded, mystified.

"He has admitted a certain interest in your direction," Derwent announced heavily. "I had not given up hope of having you turned off creditably, even at this late date, but after tonight's outrageous behavior I have grave doubts."

"Turning me off creditably?" Gillian echoed in a shriek. "Sir Eustace Pogrebin is a fat, pale slug who smells of wet dog and has damp, encroaching hands and the most pushing manner! Besides, he is ancient, and I am not having any part of him."

"Sir Eustace Pogrebin is the same age as Ronan Marlowe, and a great deal more eligible," Derwent said sharply.

"Not as far as I'm concerned."

"Do you mean to tell me you cherish hopes of Marlowe? Let me tell you, my girl, that you wouldn't be the first one to have her hopes dashed by such an unconscionable rake. He's been holding out lures to susceptible young ladies ever since he reached the age of eighteen, and I would hope he hasn't added you to his lists of conquests."

There was still a trace of champagne in Gillian's blood. "How do you know I haven't added him to *my* list of conquests?"

Derwent's mouth opened, closed, and opened again. "Do you mean to suggest he has had the temerity to make you an offer? I find that extremely difficult to believe."

"I am not considered an antidote quite yet, Derwent!"

"No, of course not," he agreed in a surprisingly soothing tone. "But you aren't in Marlowe's line at all. However, if he has made you an offer, it behooves me to meet with him and—"

"You know perfectly well he has not," she said abruptly, disliking the smug gleam in his small dark eyes.

"And I know perfectly well that you have too good an idea of what is due your name and your family even to countenance such impertinence," he said. "And I trust you won't forget again."

"Hmmph," replied Gillian in an unencouraging manner.

"My dear." He tried a more placating tone in the face of her response. "What in the world made you do anything so foolish? When you know how much we would dislike the connection?"

"*I* do not dislike the connection," she said flatly. "And I was celebrating my thirtieth birthday, something my family quite forgot to do."

Derwent had the grace to look abashed. "You should have told me," he accused.

"I did. Several times. But believe me, brother dear, I enjoyed myself far more this evening than I would have closeted with you and Letty!" With that bit of pleasurable impertinence she turned her back on him and sailed up the stairs.

"Did he ring a rare peal over you?" Felicity was awaiting her in the small, comfortable bedroom that had been allotted the maiden aunt, an anxious expression on her pretty face as she sat cross-legged on Gilly's bed, a shawl around her thin night rail.

Gillian found herself unaccountably relieved and amused. "Well, he tried to do so," she admitted, seating herself at her dressing table and beginning to divest herself of her diamonds. "But I refused to let him."

"You *refused* to let him?" she echoed, aghast.

"Absolutely. I was not in the mood to be bullied," she said blithely, eyeing her reflection with a critical eye. Her thick, tawny hair framed her face quite nicely in the new style, she had to admit. And the glowing eyes, the bright cheeks, and the tremulous mouth did not come amiss either. Why, she really was quite pretty. And Marlowe was right, her face was as smooth and unlined as Felicity's. She swung her head wonderingly, and the diamonds flashed in the candlelight. Sir Eustace Pogrebin, indeed.

"I am so terribly sorry I told him where you were," Felicity was saying, unaware of her aunt's inattention. "But they woke me up on the drawing room sofa and I just blurted it out. I tried to . . ." her voice trailed off. "Where did you get those earrings?"

Gilly met her niece's eyes in the mirror. "Earrings?" she echoed innocently. "Why, I've always had them."

"What a bouncer! Those are the same earbobs we saw in the jeweler's shop that day with Lord Marlowe. Don't tell me you went back there yourself and bought them," she accused.

"Well, I won't tell you that, since it would be untrue."

"That hasn't stopped you before. Where did you get them?" demanded Felicity. "You weren't wearing them when you left."

"You weren't in any state to notice anything when we left," her aunt said tartly. "And how in the world you knew where we were when you were sound asleep long before we made our plans . . ."

"I wasn't quite asleep," Felicity admitted sheepishly. "I was just resting my eyes. I knew perfectly well that you wouldn't have gone without me, nor with me, for that matter. And I wanted you to go out and celebrate on your birthday," she said virtuously.

"Well, that is extremely kind of you, Felicity, but . . ."

"Don't change the subject. Where did you get those earbobs?"

"They were a birthday present."

"Whomever from? No one in the family remembered . . ." Felicity stopped, her eyes wide with sudden comprehension. "Oh, merciful heavens, you don't mean Marlowe himself . . . ?"

They *were* pretty earrings, Gillian thought idly. "Indeed, I do mean Lord Marlowe himself."

"He gave them to you?"

Gillian nodded.

"And you accepted them?" Again Gilly nodded, and Felicity let out a rude whistle of amazement. "But Gilly, a lady never accepts such a gift from a gentleman unless he is a member of her immediate family. Does Papa know?"

"Of course not. And you aren't to tell him," Gilly said fiercely. "It doesn't mean anything. Lord Marlowe is a trifle eccentric, and he wished me to have these earrings. I tried to refuse, but then I decided that would be foolishly churlish of me. But that doesn't mean anyone has to know where they came from."

"Gilly, you are becoming devious."

Gillian sighed happily. "I suppose I am."

"Gilly?" There was a troubled note in Felicity's voice.

"Yes, my sweet?"

"You . . . you aren't in love with Lord Marlowe, are you?" she inquired anxiously, pleating her night rail with distracted fingers as she surveyed her surprising aunt.

"In love?" Gillian's laugh was creditable. "Have you been reading romantic novels again?"

"And who was it started me on them?" Felicity shot back. "You haven't answered my question."

Gillian didn't really wish to take off the earbobs that Ronan Marlowe had placed so deftly in her ears, but she could scarcely sleep with them tangling in her hair. Removing them with seemingly unconcerned dispatch, she refused to meet her niece's accusing eyes. "Don't be absurd, Felicity. Lord Marlowe has been all that is charming, and I must admit it feeds my consequence to have such an eligible parti paying me compliments. But I am past the age of romance, my dear."

"I don't believe you."

"Don't you? I assure you, I am not lying," she lied blithely. "I look on Lord Marlowe as an elderly version of your cousin Bertie. With a bit more sense, I might add."

Felicity was still unconvinced, and Gillian judged it time to change the subject to one closer to her volatile niece's heart. "You haven't told me how you and Mr. Blackstone are getting along. I presume that was where you were yesterday afternoon?"

The ploy succeeded. "We aren't getting along well at all," she said darkly, biting her lip. "He seems to think he's not good enough for me. That he can't provide me with fancy dresses and jewels and parties. As if I cared for such trumpery stuff!"

"You seem to have been fairly attached to such trumpery stuff anytime these past few months," Gillian pointed out in a kindly tone.

"Well, if I had Liam I wouldn't have to fill my time with such fustian," Felicity replied, and Gillian was inclined to believe her. "But will he listen? Of course not. Men always think they know best what will make women happy."

"Occasionally they do," Gilly observed, eyeing the ear-bobs fondly.

"Perhaps," Felicity conceded. "But not this time. Liam insists that he won't take me away from the only kind of life I've ever known. I shall simply have to convince him that the life I'm leading is far less preferable to one with him, despite the hardships he envisions."

Like Felicity's maid before her, Gillian was filled with dread. "Whatever do you have in mind?" she inquired faintly.

"I haven't decided yet. But something suitably daring to convince Liam that a life with him would be much better than the sinful ways one could get into in society."

"Sinful?" she echoed, aghast.

"Well, not precisely sinful. I haven't made up my mind. But if you're certain you have no interest in Lord Marlowe, he might prove just the thing. If Liam thought I was about to be compromised by a gazetted rake, I don't doubt he'd make some move to stop it."

"Felicity, it wouldn't do to underestimate Lord Marlowe. I don't think he's a person to make a may-game of," Gillian stammered.

"You needn't worry, Gilly. I can take care of myself. Unlike my sweet-natured aunt." Leaning down, she gave her aunt a careless kiss good night. "Happy thirtieth birthday, Gilly. I promise I shall devise a suitable gift to mark the occasion, even if it is a trifle late." She disappeared out the door, leaving Gillian prey to the greatest misgivings.

It was without question that her sweet-natured aunt was unable to take care of herself. Else she would never have allowed herself to be closeted in that sumptuous back room with a man of Marlowe's address and reputation. Never would have accepted the beautiful diamond ear-bobs, and most certainly never would have allowed him to kiss her in that devastating fashion. Or kissed him back so enthusiastically.

Of course, she could always blame the champagne. But she knew perfectly well, deep in her heart of hearts, that that excuse wouldn't hold water. It was with a troubled expression that Gillian crawled into bed just as dawn was streaking the dark sky with purple and rose. As she stared out into the night she found herself wondering where Ronan Marlowe was at that moment. Had he found another, less innocent lady to share his midnight supper of lobster and champagne? Or had he stayed alone in that room, thinking of her with a melancholy air? While the latter was distinctly preferable, Gillian was far too practical to hope such a thing had happened. No doubt he was lying in that gold-hung bed she had glimpsed, sound asleep, his conscience untroubled by any memory of his earlier visitor. The thought was disturbingly enticing— not his untroubled conscience, but the image of his long, lean body stretched out on what would undoubtedly be satin sheets. She wondered what he wore when he slept.

"Damn," she said aloud, abruptly swearing off champagne for the rest of her life. Shutting her eyes to the lightening sky, she drifted off into a troubled sleep, the diamond earbobs clutched in her hand.

LORD MARLOWE WAS neither in bed nor asleep. As a matter of fact, he was doing exactly what Gillian would have wished. He was sitting alone in his rooms at the gaming salon, a glass of brandy in one slim, long-fingered hand, an abstracted expression on his dark face. And he was contemplating Gillian Redfern.

"So this is where you are." Vivian's voice drifted from the doorway. His reddened nose and watery eyes attested to a night of deep drinking, and his empty pockets and peevish temper attested to the quality of his luck at the faro tables. "I wondered where you had gotten to. I thought I'd lost my wager tonight. It's all of a piece, though. The luck has been damnable lately."

"You haven't lost your wager yet, Viv." Marlowe stirred himself. "That's not to say you won't, but it's far more enjoyable stretching it out."

"It seems to me the chit is about ready to be plucked," he observed.

"The *lady*, Viv," Marlowe corrected in a lazy tone that held a note of steel, "is absurdly vulnerable. But our bet is not about her eventual plucking, like some ripe piece of fruit. Our wager is simply whether she will be ready to compromise herself for me."

"I would think you had already won," Viv sneered.

"You forget that the lady *is* a lady. And a Redfern. Sister of Derwent Redfern. I don't doubt she has strong misgivings about a rackety sort like me. And I have no intention of having her think I might offer for her. That would be cheating."

"You think you can have her accept a slip on the shoulder? With that famous charm of yours?"

"I don't doubt it. She'll accept it, but I have no intention of collecting on her acceptance. Only on our little wager."

There was an unreadable expression on Vivian's face as he heard the unwelcome words. "Don't fancy her much, do you? She's a well enough looking piece, especially tonight. But there's no accounting for tastes." He belched politely.

"I find Miss Redfern quite delightful," Marlowe replied repressively, draining his brandy glass.

"Then if you like her so much, why don't you offer her marriage? You could always change your mind. And you've got to get leg-shackled sometime."

"No."

"Why ever not?" There was real curiosity in the watery eyes.

"I don't think that's any of your concern, Viv," he said, his amiable tone taking a part, but not all, of the sting out of the snub. "Suffice it to say that I intend to free Miss Redfern of the odious constraints of society and then to hand her over to a far more eligible parti."

"I would have thought a wealthy marquis would be extremely eligible, despite a somewhat shady reputation."

Marlowe cocked an eye at him. "Appearances can be deceiving."

"You don't mind if I write the precise nature of this wager down, do you?" Vivian continued, a sly expression on his dissipated face. "My poor brain gets so fuddled I quite often forget the particulars."

"I would rather not."

"Oh, you may keep the paper. Wouldn't want for it to fall into the wrong hands, don't you know. But really, Ronan, you can't refuse me this. Unless you prefer to cry off from the entire wager?"

Marlowe hesitated for only a moment. "No, I don't wish to cry off. Very well, Viv. But we'll keep the paper in my safe at Bruton Street. I don't want anyone having access to it."

"Of course not. It would spoil our wager," Vivian agreed roundly.

The look of suspicion in Marlowe's eyes was masked. "Exactly so," he said gently, and reached for a pen and paper.

# Chapter Ten

IT WAS ELEVEN o'clock before Gillian opened her sleepy blue eyes once more, and then it was only under duress. A disgustingly cheerful Felicity bounced into her room unannounced, flinging open the curtains and greeting her muzzy-headed aunt with what the poor, benighted creature could only consider wickedly unfeeling volume.

"Mama has sent me to rouse you, Gilly," she announced brightly. "I gather Papa forbore to tell her of your activities last night, and she has already had to endure a visit from the cook, demanding this week's menus, another visit from the children's governess, who has given her notice, and we've only had this poor creature less than a fortnight. And then the children descended with their usual lively spirits, with Jeremy smearing jam all over Mama's new dress. And Papa left the house in a thunderous mood, and now Mrs. Huddleston and her loathsome daughter Prunella have arrived, subjecting poor Mama to all sorts of inquisitions. So you'd best come rescue her, or you'll never hear the end of it."

"Cannot your mama," Gillian demanded in a plaintive whisper to accommodate the pounding in her head, "manage her household for one morning? She must do it when I am off visiting Pamela or Eunice."

"No, she doesn't. Everytime you leave she succumbs to a severe spasm of the nerves which requires her to keep to her bedroom with no visitors, while she subsists on an invalid's diet of beef tea and caramel creams."

Gillian laughed, then regretted it as her head took exception to the noise. "You are an amazingly undutiful child," she chided, throwing back the covers and pulling herself wearily to her feet.

"Not undutiful," Felicity protested. "I came up here immediately when I noticed Mama's look of fretful panic. I am merely accustomed to her little ways."

"Honor thy father and thy mother," Gillian quoted, rummaging in her closet for something uncomplicated to wear.

"Well, I do, whenever they do anything worth honoring," Felicity said frankly. "Flossie's on her way. I caught her in the second pantry with the footman. You'll have to watch the girl, Gilly. We can't have her sneaking off with every handsome man she sees."

Gillian's busy hands stopped as she blushed a deep red. "You're absolutely right," she said in a muffled tone.

"Oh, Gilly, don't be absurd!" her niece said in stricken tones. "I didn't mean you."

"No, you are very wise. It doesn't do for any poor female to allow herself to be persuaded by the male sex into unbecoming behavior," she said in a strangled voice.

"Balderdash! Your behavior last night was becoming in the extreme. You have only to look in the mirror."

"Don't willfully misunderstand me, Felicity. I . . ." Before she could finish her wrathful sentence her pert niece was out the door with a flounce of her pale yellow skirts. Shaking her head ruefully, Gillian attempted to put herself into some semblance of order, with belated assistance from her breathless, red-faced maid, Flossie.

When she entered the puce drawing room that was Letty's favorite and even in the best of times made Gillian feel faintly bilious, she wished she could have taken a bit longer. Mrs. Huddleston was still holding forth, her raddled cheeks, beaklike nose, and beady, curious eyes filling Gillian with a sinking feeling. Miss Prunella Huddleston, her only unmarried daughter, was looking similarly curious, and indeed, with the same unprepossessing features as her mama, down to the thin lips and pointed chin, the sight was not aesthetically pleasing to a lady suffering from the effects of a night of overindulgence.

"How delightful to see you again," Mrs. Huddleston boomed forth, and Gillian nearly wept at the pounding of her head. "Prunella was just expressing great interest as to where you were, weren't you, my dear?" Miss Prunella had been masking her interest admirably. "It's been an age since we've seen you, Gillian dear. You haven't changed a bit—the years have been very kind."

Gritting her teeth, Gillian deposited a kiss on Letty's plump, sulking cheek and smiled faintly at the two unwelcome visitors. "How thoughtful of you to visit Letty," she said in her soft voice. "I am sure she has many times wished she could see more of you."

Letty set her sullen face into an unconvincing smile as she nodded agreement. "I was just saying so to dear Mrs. Huddleston," she agreed, and only Gillian could recognize the edge in her plaintive tones. "You interrupted us in the midst of the most fascinating conversation, Gillian."

Grasping at straws, Gillian said quickly, "Oh, forgive me. I'll just leave . . ."

"Sit down, Gillian." The note of steel in Letty's voice was not well disguised, and the sharp-eyed Prunella eyed the sisters-in-law with avid delight. Gillian sat, accepting her fate with stoic forbearance.

"We were discussing the new Lord Marlowe," Mrs. Huddleston explained with what she no doubt considered charming condescension. "I was asking dear Letty if she knew anything about the man. All sorts of rumors have been flying, and after all, I believe the two of them were rather well acquainted some twenty years ago."

Gillian stared at her portly sister-in-law with undisguised fascination. "Oh, really? I had no idea, Letty."

"I haven't seen the man since he was sent away by his family," she snapped with more energy than Gillian had seen her exhibit in many a year. "I should hope he had abandoned some of his more ramshackle ways."

"I think it highly unlikely, despite the respect he owes to the title he never deserved," Mrs. Huddleston said repressively. "The man has set up a gaming hell, Letty."

"I had heard something to that effect."

"And my husband has heard there are all sorts of wicked goings-on. Gambling for outrageous stakes, estates changing hands on the turn of a card."

"Surely that is nothing new," said Letty, reaching for a bonbon from the silver dish just in reach of her plump white fingers. "White's and Watier's have been operating in such a manner for years."

"But my husband says there is a question of dishonesty in the play. And that certain people, people highly connected with the place, have developed the habit of luring green young men there and fleecing them shamelessly. Horace wouldn't tell me where he heard it, but it was *the* most reliable source."

"I would have thought *the* most reliable source would be Lord Marlowe himself," Gillian snapped, unable to keep silent any longer. Those beady little eyes turned toward her, and she felt a sense of impending doom.

"I wouldn't know, my dear. But then, Horace is not unconvinced."

"Well, if he has such ignoble suspicions why does he continue to frequent the place?" Gillian inquired.

"Because he has no proof. And for some odd reason he likes Marlowe. Gentlemen have ever been incomprehensible. How one could like and admire a man that one suspects of shaving the cards and fleecing innocents is beyond me. And as for Marlowe's licentious behavior . . . well, the less said about that the better."

"Amen!" agreed Gillian in a determined tone.

Mrs. Huddleston looked nonplussed for a moment, then ploughed on, undefeated. "His opera dancers are legion. Never has the same one been in his keeping for more than a few weeks. He has been flirting and casting out lures to all sorts of ladies of good reputation, and then, once he has raised hopes in their breasts, he has dropped them and moved on to another." She sniffed. "Thank heavens he knew better than to trifle with my sweet Prunella."

Her sweet Prunella did not look similarly gratified at Marlowe's forbearance. "But that's not all, Mama," she said in her whining voice. "Tell them about last night."

All Gillian's forebodings came home to roost. "Last night?" she echoed with an admirable attempt at innocence.

"Last night," Mrs. Huddleston said in awesome tones, "a lady visited Marlowe's gaming hell. And remained closeted alone with the lecherous beast for almost half an hour!" The sharp eyes left Gillian little doubt they knew perfectly well who that lady had been.

"I don't know what you're making such a piece of work over this for," Letty said fretfully, her understanding not being great. "Any number of ladies must frequent Marlowe's salon. Sally Jersey has been there and tells me it's monstrously entertaining."

"I mean a *lady*, Letty. Someone of heretofore unblemished reputation. Someone we know quite well." Two pairs of Huddleston eyes were glaring at poor Gillian, and Letty, a bit slow on the uptake but not beyond hope, finally followed the direction of their accusatory gaze to Gillian's flushed face.

"Good gracious," she breathed. "You don't mean . . . ?"

"She does," replied Gillian, throwing her shoulders back.

"Good gracious," Letty said again, resorting to another chocolate in her agitation. "I don't know what Derwent will say to all this."

"Derwent has already said a great deal about it," Gillian assured her calmly, controlling her temper with an effort. "He escorted me home from Marlowe's salon. Mrs. Huddleston forgot to tell you that, and also forgot to mention that I was accompanied by Bertie."

"Who promptly abandoned you to that—that libertine's attentions," Mrs. Huddleston stated, her thin nose pinched in disapproval. "I have regretted coming here with such distressing news, Letty dear, but I believe I know my duty when it lies before me."

"I cannot thank you enough, Mrs. Huddleston," Letty breathed. "If I had only realized Gillian was capable of such . . ."

Gillian rose to her full height. "Not that I think my presence is having a constraining effect," she broke in affably, "but I'm certain you will be a great deal more comfortable castigating me without having me here. I promised I would escort Felicity to Hookhams."

"More novels!" Letty shrieked, incensed. "You'll be getting more novels, and I blame them for your current licentious behavior!" She blithely ignored the stack of French romances that lay beside her own bed next to the tray of chocolate creams.

"I will be certain, however, that Felicity only reads improving tales, Letty," Gillian replied politely. "It is always a pleasure to see you both, Mrs. Huddleston. Prunella." With that she sailed out of the drawing room, leaving more than one lady gasping in outrage.

"BUT I HAVE NOT the slightest desire to go to Hookham's Lending Library," Felicity argued as she kept pace with her aunt's determined progress down the crowded London streets. "I have more than enough to read, and I was rather hoping I would have a chance to get down to see Liam this afternoon."

"There'll be time enough for that," Gillian said grimly. "And as a matter of fact, I have more than enough to read myself. I merely had to leave the house before I did physical violence on that wicked old toad."

"Mama?" Felicity inquired, surprised.

"Mrs. Huddleston. She arrived this morning with the express purpose of telling Letty where I had been last night. I left the three of them tearing my character to shreds when I could bear it no longer. They were just jealous because Lord Marlowe paid no attention to that bracket-faced daughter of hers. I should have known something like this would happen. I should have never left Winchester, no matter how insupportable I find Pamela's husband."

"Now, now, Gilly, don't be absurd. Then you wouldn't have met Lord Marlowe."

"Exactly!"

"And you wouldn't have those unsuitable diamond ear-bobs that I would give anything for," Felicity pointed out. "You would be safe and secure and bored to death!"

"I hadn't noticed I was bored before," Gillian said stiffly without a great deal of veracity.

"Well, I had. And I think Lord Marlowe's been very good for you. As long as you remain heart-whole, as you insist you will, I can only think it an excellent thing. You wanted some shaking up."

"Not that I noticed," Gillian snapped irritably, her head still pounding somewhat from last night's exertions. "Are you coming in with me?"

"I thought I might wait out here. It's such a delightful day I hate to miss any of this glorious sunshine," Felicity said innocently.

Unfortunately Gillian was too preoccupied to notice this unusual affinity for Mother Nature on the part of her niece. Besides, the aforementioned glorious sunshine was contributing to the monstrous headache.

"You know perfectly well you shouldn't be out here alone. But I suppose it is useless to try to stop you. I don't suppose Letty has any faith in my chaperoning abilities anymore."

"I don't suppose she does," Felicity agreed cheerfully.

"Hmmph!" Gillian was too weary and irritable to argue further. "I'll be out directly. I know precisely what I want, and I don't doubt they will not have it. Do not talk to strangers, Felicity."

It took Gillian rather longer to find the book she was seeking, an unusual treatise on lives of monkish contemplation, but at last success was hers. With a feeling of foreboding, the leather-bound volume in her hand, she dashed out the door, her sharp eyes searching the street for her ingenuous niece.

With a sinking feeling Gillian finally discovered her, slender arm entwined through a gentleman's strong, broadcloth one, her pretty face smiling up as she chattered on at breakneck pace, her eyes fluttering up in a manner that Gillian had come to recognize as Felicity Flirting.

"Blast!" she said under her breath, weaving her way through the passersby on the way to her niece's rescue. "I cannot leave the child alone for a moment. She's even worse than I am."

She was almost upon them when Felicity turned, greeting her aunt with innocent charm as she retained her grip on the gentleman's arm. "Aunt Gillian!" she cried. "Look who I have found this morning. Was there ever such a fortunate happenstance?"

The tall figure turned, the arm tried to detach itself from Felicity's limpet grip, and Ronan Blakely, Lord Marlowe, bowed with his customary grace, the faint trace of a quizzical smile in his dark green eyes.

# Chapter Eleven

"GOOD MORNING, Miss Redfern," he greeted her, and his slow, deep voice sent an uncomfortable little thrill along Gillian's backbone as well as a deep blush to her suddenly pale complexion. There was no way she could banish from her mind the circumstances in which she had last seen Ronan Marlowe, especially with that wicked, knowing smile lurking in the back of his fine green eyes.

"Why, Gilly, you're blushing," Felicity announced ingenuously, and Gillian controlled a strong urge to trample on her foot. "Whatever happened to overset you?"

"Miss Redfern doesn't appear to be the slightest bit discomposed," Marlowe broke in smoothly. "As a matter of fact, she is looking absolutely radiant this morning considering the excesses of last night."

"Excesses?" Felicity echoed, her high, breathless laugh that was also a key part of Felicity flirting grating suddenly on Gillian's already frayed nerves.

"An excess of champagne, Felicity," she said casually as she felt the color subside from her face. "Good morning, Lord Marlowe."

"Lord Marlowe was just telling me the most fascinating stories of his life on the Continent," Felicity continued archly. "I vow, I have never laughed so much in my entire life. What a vastly diverting life you have led, my lord." She batted her eyes at him outrageously.

"No more than most," he replied shortly, struggling once more to release himself from her clinging grip and this time succeeding. "Miss Redfern . . ."

Felicity recaptured his arm. "I am convinced you are too modest," she interrupted. "I have it on the best authority that you are a rake, forever casting out lures to hapless females and then abandoning them once their hopes have been raised."

Marlowe's dark face showed a flash of interest. "And who told you that? I hope it wasn't your aunt?" The green eyes rested on Gillian's discomfited expression.

Felicity laughed again, and Gillian's mortification rose. "Oh, heavens, no! Gilly does nothing but sing your praises, although she says she sees you as a slightly older version of Bertie."

"She does, does she?" He appeared to be more amused than affronted, but Gilly by this time had had enough.

"Felicity!" she said in a dangerous undertone, taking that lady's arm in an iron grip and removing her from Lord Marlowe's side. "Your behavior goes beyond the line of what is pleasing!"

"But I haven't spoken a word that wasn't true, have I?" she demanded with a great show of innocence. "Didn't you say Lord Marlowe reminded you of Cousin Bertie?"

"Yes, do answer, Miss Redfern," Marlowe encouraged her affably. "I wasn't aware that I appeared to you in quite so callow a light."

Gilly's deepening blush was reply enough. "Anything I might have said to my niece was not meant to be repeated," she said in a muffled tone. "I . . ."

"You see!" Felicity interrupted once more, and Gilly longed to strangle her. "I would never have made up such a thing. For my part I think she must have windmills in her head, my lord. I find you vastly romantic. But then, Gilly is of an age where she has ceased to have an interest in such things."

Marlowe raised an eyebrow, and the effect was to make him appear even more saturnine. "Oh, really? I had failed to notice such a disinterest on your aunt's part, but then, I may have deceived myself."

"I do wish," Gilly said finally, "that the two of you would cease to discuss me as if I weren't here. Leave go of his lordship's arm, Felicity, and let us return to Berkeley Square. I have a great deal to say to you about your unbecoming behavior."

"You see what an ogre she is?" Felicity demanded of Marlowe, releasing his arm with a great show of reluctance. "Dare I ask you to come to my rescue and save me from the lecture her disapproving expression promises? Believe me, despite her gentle appearance she can be quite fierce."

Marlowe turned his shoulder to her, smiling down at Gillian in a manner that left her feeling curiously weak-kneed. "Your niece is certainly an ill-mannered minx," he remarked, not even bothering to lower his voice. "Is there any way we can dispense with her tiresome company, or do you need her as a chaperone?"

Felicity's outraged gasp coincided with Gilly's reluctant chuckle. "I am afraid the shoe is on the other foot, my lord. I am Felicity's chaperone, and could hardly let her out by herself."

"I can see why. Very well, I suppose we must make do with what chance has offered us. I shall see you home by way of Gunters, and we may only hope that the ices offered there will keep her prattle-box busy enough to allow us to enjoy a brief conversation." He held out his arm for her, and after a moment's hesitation she took it.

Felicity's discomfiture could only last a certain time. Undaunted, she caught his other arm in her confiding clasp and smiled up at him winningly. "I will behave myself," she said with a twinkle in her eye. "If you have the remarkably good taste to prefer my aunt to myself, I can hardly fault you. But let me tell you you are setting all my carefully laid plans to naught."

If she hoped to beguile Marlowe with her honesty, she had failed once more. "Just as well," he said repressively. "If you behave yourself we will allow you to accompany us. If you keep chattering I will, despite your aunt's protests, bundle you into a hackney and send you back to Berkeley Square. Is that understood?" There was a flinty note in his voice, and Felicity, usually a sunny-tempered girl, for a moment lost her customary amiability.

"Certainly," she snapped. "Though why you should be so uncivil . . ."

"It is no wonder you feel fagged to death if you have to put up with her all the time," Marlowe said to Gillian, who had been surveying this interchange with amazement and not a little gratification at seeing her irrepressible niece silenced for once. Felicity had subsided into a very pretty case of the sulks, and Gilly cast her an anxious look before replying.

"I love Felicity more than anything," she defended her. "Admittedly she is a trifle high-spirited . . ."

"I don't wish to talk about your niece," Marlowe interrupted gently. "I wanted to find out how you fared after last night. Derwent Redfern can be exceedingly unpleasant, and I have the notion you aren't terribly adept at taking care of yourself."

Gilly's blush deepened as she was startled into a laugh. "How can you say such a thing?" she demanded with the trace of a smile in her warm blue eyes. "I would have thought I had proved to you last night how very capable I was."

"You proved a great many things last evening, my dear Gilly," he said softly. "Not the least of which is how delightfully innocent you are. But I wouldn't want you to suffer for last night, as I have little doubt that idiot of a brother of yours would like to make you."

"That is my father you are insulting," Felicity interrupted, clearly fascinated by this exchange.

"I am fully aware of that. I am also aware that I told you to be quiet. If you do not do so I will be forced to believe that you resemble your esteemed father even more than I had believed."

"You are—are a monster!" Felicity stormed.

Marlowe laughed heartlessly. "I would think you would be gratified to know that you resembled the father you are so busy defending. Though I will grant you that there is a look of your mother about you also."

"You know my mother?" Felicity questioned, curiosity overlaying her outrage.

"Far too well," he replied enigmatically before turning back to the lady on his other arm. "Was he unbearably stuffy last night? I wished I had confronted him."

"That would have only made things worse. And no, he wasn't too desperately awful. I simply told him I wasn't in the mood to be yelled at. He was so astounded he was scarcely able to come out with one or two lecture points before I escaped to bed."

"You don't usually stand up to him?" There was a pleased expression on his face that Gilly couldn't quite fathom.

"Not usually," she admitted. "However, I decided that at the advanced age of thirty I was far too old to be intimidated."

"May I hope I added to your feelings of resolution?"

A smile played around Gilly's soft mouth, and the expression in Marlowe's eyes deepened inexplicably. "You may hope so," she said, giving nothing away.

He stared down at her for a long moment. "Can't we dispense with your niece's presence?" he demanded in a husky voice. "I would much prefer to continue our conversation of last night in private."

"I don't believe that conversation will be continued, my lord. I was a trifle above myself last night from an excess of champagne and high spirits. I doubt it will happen again."

"I am grieved to hear you say so. I have yet to see a case where high spirits can truly be described as excessive, and champagne is such a delightful drink. However, if you are determined to continue a nunlike existence . . ."

"I am determined to do no such thing," she shot back. "I merely have regained a sense of propriety . . ."

"Worse and worse. I had thought better of you, Gillyflower," he said softly, and Gillian's resolution almost failed.

"I am exceedingly flattered," she said firmly, "at your offers to lead me astray, but I believe I have other obligations. Not the least of which is to my niece. I am supposed to provide a model of proper behavior for her, not an example of flighty womanhood bent upon her own destruction."

"And is that how you see yourself with me?" he queried curiously, apparently unmoved by her rejection. "You think that I would destroy you?"

"Oh, I don't doubt you would regret it tremendously. But not enough to leave me alone. And destroyed I certainly will be, unless you do so."

He stood motionless for a long, silent moment, staring down at her with an unreadable expression on his dark face. "There is more than one definition of destruction, Gilly. Some would call a blameless life sacrificed on the altar of family duty destruction, but I will have to leave it up to you. If you should ever change your mind you know where to find me." Abruptly he released their arms, and with a graceful, mocking little bow, he left them, striding down Bond Street without a backward glance, leaving the two Redfern ladies staring after his tall, elegant figure with amazed chagrin.

"I admire your resolve, Gilly," Felicity said after a long moment, and her voice was subdued. "I certainly could never have sent him away."

"I wasn't precisely aware that I had done so," Gilly admitted ruefully. "But I can only be thankful that he has been so easily discouraged. No doubt it will save me a great deal of future embarrassment." If she looked rather more shattered than thankful, her niece exercised her infrequent tact and forbore to mention it.

"I suppose this means we must forgo Gunters?" she inquired innocently. Sweets were Felicity's downfall, and despite her slender curves she was able to consume a startling amount, almost rivaling her once-slender mother.

With a belated start Gilly pulled her scattered wits together. "I should say so! I have no intention of rewarding you for today's behavior. You will kindly explain to me, Felicity, the reason for your inexplicably vulgar behavior, clinging to Lord Marlowe's arm like that, and being so very pushing! I could scarcely believe it."

Felicity shrugged. "I thought I might excite his interest. If Liam knew that such a desperate character was casting out lures to me, he might relent and run away to Gretna Green."

"Felicity, dearest!" Gillian shook her head sadly. "You have no sense whatsoever. Lord Marlowe would never be taken in by such obvious measures."

"He most certainly would have been, if he wasn't so busy staring at you. And despite your protests, I never in my life saw a more jealous expression on anyone than on your face when you came out and saw us together. I thought you told me you had no interest in him."

"I lied," she admitted flatly. "And do not think you may repeat that, for I will only lie again. I am old enough to know better, and if I have a trace of romantic weakness then I don't doubt but what your mother is right, and that it comes from reading too many French novels."

"That was a curious thing he said about Mama, was it not?" Felicity mused. "About knowing her far too well? What do you suppose he could have meant by that?"

"I have no idea, and I don't suppose we shall have the chance to find out. I shouldn't expect to see Lord Marlowe again, except from a distance. I can congratulate myself on having made my feelings clear to him," she said mournfully.

Felicity smiled, feeling suddenly far wiser than her innocent aunt. "Actually, I think he's full aware of your feelings, Gilly. And I have little doubt we shall be seeing him again, very soon."

"Well, then, I shall simply have to stiffen my resolve. I cannot allow myself to grow too fond of him." She put a hand to her head. "It must be this wretched headache that makes me feel so unhappy."

"Headaches will do that every time," her niece agreed, suppressing a smile. "If you care to rest this afternoon, I will endeavor to make sure that everyone leaves you alone."

"That would be lovely," Gillian sighed. "I find there is nothing I long for more than a few hours' peace and quiet so that I can rest and reflect."

"And shed a few private tears?" Felicity suggested.

"Don't be absurd. I have nothing to cry for," Gillian replied sharply, feeling quite desperately sorry for herself. "Indeed, I cannot imagine a more fortunate creature in all of London." She strode on ahead, ignoring her niece's knowing smile, keeping her head high all the way to the Redfern mansion.

# Chapter Twelve

NO SOONER HAD Felicity managed to get the miserable Gillian safely ensconced in the fastness of her bedroom than she leaped into action. With the muffled sounds of Gilly's strangled tears in the back of her head, she stripped off her fashionable pale primrose dress and attired herself in her plainest dark brown frock. The riot of dark curls she pinned severely to her head, the thin kid slippers were replaced by sturdy leather boots. There was nothing she could do about her shining blue eyes or the flushed complexion that contributed to her notable beauty, but then she was counting on those assets to work in her favor. This would be Liam's last chance before she put her desperate plan into motion. To be sure, Lord Marlowe had proven tiresomely uncooperative, but she hadn't despaired of achieving some good for her aunt out of the ensuing melee. If Liam and her parents forced her into it, of course.

Wednesday was a busy day for all classes of London society. Not only was it the day for Almack's tedious subscription balls, it was also the day Mr. Blackstone's mission provided free soup and stale bread to whomever sought it—the only day that Felicity could be reasonably sure of a welcome. She wasn't about to wait another week to find out how bold she must be, and she wasn't about to have her maid Marjorie trailing along behind her. Desperate times called for desperate measures, and Felicity was ready.

It proved slightly more difficult obtaining a hackney without a servant to attend to it. More than one sped by her, spraying her with dust and mud and heaven knew what else and forcing her to jump to safety at the last minute. Finally one driver took pity on her woebegone state and pretty face. The conveyance smelled of stale cigars and cabbage, the seat was frayed, with springs sticking into her anatomy no matter how she shifted. But a light rain had begun to fall, despite the earlier sunshine, and Felicity leaned back gratefully, breathing through her mouth and holding a lawn handkerchief to her nostrils. The smell at the mission would be far worse, but it always took her a bit to get used to it.

Liam was nowhere in sight when she entered the crowded confines of the mission. A disreputable old slattern with the unpromising name of Leaky Sal greeted Felicity with the ease of an old acquaintance.

"Looking for 'is nibs, are ye?" She wiped her nose on her filthy sleeve and pointed with the soup ladle. "Happen he's in the back storage room. He didn't tell me you were coming."

"He didn't know."

"He's not too happy, miss. Some high and mighty types have been ferretin' around all day long. Left just a short while ago, but he isn't happy. Not one bit, he ain't. You might see if you can cheer 'im up."

"I'll do my best, Sal," she promised, hanging Marjorie's second-best cloak on the peg provided and heading off in search of her true love.

The dim confines of the small room directly behind the kitchens were illuminated with the sparse light of the rain-drenched afternoon as it fought its way through the spotless window high up on one wall. Liam's back, tall and straight and infinitely dear, was turned to her as she entered the room on silent feet. She shut the warped door behind her with a quiet click that made him whirl around, and for a moment his expression was all she could have hoped for. Naked love and longing were on his handsome face, and a look of such joy in his usually anguished eyes as he took an involuntary step toward her, his arms outstretched.

It was all the encouragement she needed. "Liam," she breathed, and ran into his arms before he could drop them in sudden guilty remorse.

The feel of her soft, warm body against his was far too much for one of his sternly repressed, passionate nature. With a groan of despair his arms went around her, and his mouth came down on hers in a kiss of such burning desire that Felicity's scattered intellect deserted her completely, and she melted against him willingly, too caught up in the tide of their passion to demur. Until, with a groan, Liam suddenly thrust her away from him.

"How could I?" he demanded of himself, his beautiful voice filled with loathing as he straightened his collar. "How could I be so led astray by my bestial passions? And I, a man of the cloth?"

"I would hardly call them bestial passions," Felicity said huffily, pulling the once demure neckline of her dress up. "It's entirely normal. You love me. I love you. Why shouldn't we . . . ?"

"It's shameful! We cannot marry. Your father has refused his consent, and rightly so. We could hardly afford to live on the pittance I earn, even if your father was disposed to look charitably upon my suit. We know we must deny ourselves, and yet what did I do? I was so overcome by my animal nature that I allowed myself to forget every vestige of propriety."

"I wish you'd stop talking about animals," Felicity said feelingly, her upset stemming more from frustrated passion than anything else. "You make me sound like a sow in rut."

If she hoped to shock him she did so, even though a temporary flash of humor lightened his face for a moment. "I suppose I must blame myself for that, too," he said heavily. "You know better than to use such terms."

"Fustian! You didn't used to be so prudish when you had the living in Sussex. Much good you would have been to the farm folk if you'd pokered up the moment someone mentioned the laws of nature."

"There's a great deal of difference between Leaky Sal talking about her manner of earning a living and a well-bred young lady talking about sows in rut," he snapped. "If I hadn't so forgotten myself—"

"Liam," she interrupted him, and her voice was calm and sure, her blue eyes shining in the dim afternoon light. "I love you. I only wish you'd forget yourself more often."

It would have taken a saint to rise above such encouragement, and Liam Blackstone, for all his efforts, was no saint. With a stifled groan he pulled her back into his arms, and proceeded to kiss her with a ruthless force that Felicity, for all her compliance, found immensely gratifying and just the tiniest bit frightening. A new plan was forming at the hazy edges of her consciousness, one that involved the not regrettable exigency of seduction on the storage room floor. Though who would do the seducing and who would be seduced remained to be seen. Liam had pressed her willing body back against the wall, and his hands were roaming quite delightfully over her slender young curves when the storage room door was flung open. Two men stood there in the dim light, their expressions ranging from outraged horror to tolerant amusement. Liam jumped away from Felicity as if scalded, his handsome face pale with horror.

The amused gentleman spoke first, and Felicity saw his clerical garb though a horrified haze. "Sorry to interrupt you, my boy, but there was one matter we still had to check. I wonder if we might see you in private. That is, if the lady could spare you."

"Of course, sir," Liam said hastily, thrusting Felicity behind him in a vague effort to shield her from their curious faces. "I'll be with you in just one moment."

"Outrageous!" snorted one gentleman. "I've never been so appalled in my entire life. If this is the sort of thing that goes on with our young curates, I don't know what the church is coming to."

"Don't be silly, Riddington. It's a perfectly healthy thing, and it is obvious to me that the two are in love," the first voice replied, unperturbed. "If I have no objections, I fail to see why you should."

"Riddington!" Felicity echoed in horror, unfortunately out loud, and at the sound of his name the blustery gentleman turned back and peered at her through the gloom.

"Who is it?" he demanded, as Liam tried to push Felicity's body behind him.

"I must ask that the lady's anonymity be preserved," he said desperately. "If there's to be any investigation I must bear the brunt of it. This was entirely my fault; I took advantage of the girl."

This was too much for Felicity. She could hardly hide behind him while he destroyed his career in order to protect her wicked, selfish ways. Ducking under his arm, she faced her accuser squarely. "Don't pay him any heed, Mr. Riddington. He is only trying to protect me. I sought him out—it's entirely my fault."

"Who is it? Good God, it's the Redfern girl!" Riddington exclaimed in tones of horror that possibly reached the club he frequented with her father. "I can't believe it. That a child of Derwent Redfern's would be so lost to propriety that she would—"

"That's enough, Riddington," the first gentleman spoke reprovingly. "I have little doubt that this seems far worse than it actually is. I have too much respect for a man of Mr. Blackstone's integrity to jump to insulting conclusions. You and Miss Redfern are doubtless engaged to be married."

"Yes," said Felicity eagerly.

"No," said Liam. "Her father has refused his consent."

"You see!" Riddington crowed, his face red with outrage.

"Dear, dear," said the clerical gentleman. "That does place things in a different light. And does the lady's father disapprove of you? I cannot imagine that he could."

"He feels my prospects are not good enough for his daughter," Liam said stiffly. "And indeed, he's right. I am scarcely worthy of this fine lady's attention. I had determined to remain celibate and devote my life to the poor."

"Very worthy," the kindly old gentleman soothed with a trace of a twinkle in his faded blue eyes. "But had you forgotten that Saint Paul said that if the unmarried cannot control themselves they should marry.

Better be married than burn with vain desire."

"He would put it that way," Felicity said with disgust.

"You don't care for Paul, my child?" he inquired with a trace of laughter.

"Not usually," she confessed. "But in this case I agree with the thought, even if I don't care for the way he phrases it. And so I've been trying to tell Liam."

"Enough!" Riddington stormed. "I would be failing in my duty if I let this distasteful and blasphemous conversation continue. I owe it to my friend Redfern to escort his daughter out of this—this brothel before anything more happens. Where is your maidservant, young lady?" he demanded of her.

"I came alone. And I'm not ready to leave. I wanted . . ." Before she could finish Mr. Riddington had caught her arm and began dragging her toward the door.

"Unhand her!" Liam said in a murderous voice, and everyone stared at him. "I said, take your filthy hands off her. She'll go with you if you ask, but if you don't let go of her I'll be forced to forget my orders even more than I already have and plant you a facer!" This was said between clenched teeth, and there was no doubting he meant every word of it.

"Fine talking," sneered Riddington, releasing her quickly. "Seems to me you've already forgotten what was due your position long ago."

"I will not go with him," Felicity fumed. "I need to talk with you, Liam."

"I don't need to talk with you. I have already disgraced myself and you. I won't add to it. It is my fondest hope that you never have to see my miserable face again," he said woodenly.

"But I want to!" she wailed.

The kind gentleman took her arm in his gentle grasp and led her toward the door. "Come along, my dear. Mr. Blackstone and I have a great deal to talk about. Things are not as bad as they seem. Trust in the Lord, and everything will come out all right."

"Yes, but can I trust in Mr. Riddington?" she inquired with a great deal of practicality.

"Most likely not. But I will visit your father myself and see if I can't make things a bit more acceptable to him. I have high hopes for young Mr. Blackstone."

"You are far too kind, Bishop," Liam mumbled, and Felicity stared at the unprepossessing little gentleman in belated amazement.

"Bishop?" she echoed.

"Go along with Mr. Riddington, child, while I try to talk some sense into this foolish young man."

"I only hope you can, sir," she said miserably.

He smiled at her, putting her in mind of a cheery elf. "I have been accounted to have some success in these matters," he said modestly. "Leave your young man to me. And I might add, Mr. Riddington . . ."

The large, bad-tempered man turned back with an air of disapproval. "Yes, sir?" There was a grudging respect in his voice.

"I think it might be best if you could refrain from informing Mr. Redfern where you found his daughter this afternoon. I will visit with him in a few days and acquaint him with the particulars I feel he might need to know. There is no need to burden him with other worries. I am certain we can accept Miss Redfern's promise that she won't come down here again."

"But . . ." Felicity protested, but the bishop squeezed her hand.

"You must give me your promise, my child. Surely you can see this isn't at all the thing. For you or for a man in Mr. Blackstone's position."

Guilt, an uncomfortably novel sensation, assailed Felicity as she surveyed Liam's shadowed figure. "You are right," she said quietly. "You have my word."

"Well, I don't know about that," Riddington began to bluster once more.

"If her word is good enough for me, Mr. Riddington," the bishop interrupted gently, "then it is surely good enough for you."

"You're far too trusting, Bishop," Riddington grated out. "But who am I to say I know better. I'll drop her off outside her house and keep my thoughts to myself. But I don't like it. I don't like it one tiny bit."

Neither, for that matter, did Felicity. But the bishop had such kindly eyes, and Liam appeared to be so miserable, that she resolutely put the memory of his burning kisses from her mind, accepted the elderly cleric's blessing, and followed Mr. Riddington's massive figure out into the rain-swept afternoon. And if, later that night as she lay in her bed, she relived every moment of Liam's fevered embrace, there was no one to know but herself.

# Chapter Thirteen

IT WAS A DIFFICULT week for the Redfern household. Felicity, never known for her stability of manner or great good sense, had developed the oddest habit of staring out the front drawing room windows. Whenever a visitor was heard approaching, her face would pale, she would start up in great agitation, and then she would subside into a decidedly devious silence when it proved to be someone as unexceptionable as Letty's dearest friend and fellow *malade imaginaire*, Hester Toussaint, or one of Bertie's floridly attired cronies. At other times she would sit for long hours, her pretty dark eyes filled with a faraway expression, her lips curved in a manner that, had her aunt been more observant, she would have stigmatized as decidedly sly.

Bertie himself wasn't faring much better. Paler than ever, he had even appeared to have lost interest in the extravagances of dress that had so obsessed his intellect this season. Likewise bouts of fisticuffs, cock fighting, bear baiting, curricle racing, and even gaming had suddenly ceased holding out any lure for him. The desperate expression in his eyes was strong enough, however, to penetrate even Gillian's abstraction, although his Aunt Letty remained absorbed in her own world of chocolates and migraines and French novels.

Dragging herself from her self-absorption one late afternoon, Gillian encountered first Bertie, with a grim set to his mouth and a despairing look in his brown eyes. His cravat was tied in an execrable version of The Ordinary, informing Gilly's experienced eye that here was trouble indeed.

"Bertie." She caught his arm as he attempted to pass her on the broad, curving staircase of Redfern House. "The very person I was longing to see."

He stared at her abstractedly. "I am afraid I cannot stop, Gilly. I . . . I have an appointment that I cannot miss."

"An appointment?" she inquired, not missing the guilty expression or the furtive glances toward the closed door of Derwent's study. "Surely this is a very odd time of day for an appointment. Everyone will be dressing for dinner. Including you, I hope. I was counting on you to accompany your cousin and me to the Drelincourts' tonight. Your company is usually a great deal more amusing than Derwent's, and I know your uncle would welcome a chance to cry off tonight."

Bertie shook his head, removing her gentle hold on his arm in a manner that would have been rude if he weren't so obviously beset by worry. "I'm sorry, Gilly, but I cannot. Fact of the matter is, I'm not much in the partying mood nowadays."

"Bertie, if there's any way I can help . . ." she offered anxiously. "You need only to drop a hint. I'm far from purse-pinched, and there'd be no questions asked."

His affront was monumental. "What kind of rag-bird do you think I am, Gilly?" he demanded, outraged. "I haven't gotten so far down the road to rack and ruin that I need must apply to the women in my family for rescue. Good evening, Aunt!"

"Bertie!" she called after him despairingly, but he had already vanished out the front door.

This did little to improve a humor that had been beset by the foulest, blackest moods it had ever had to endure. All week long she had waited for some sign from Marlowe, some word, some gesture. Why she should have expected it she couldn't quite say, considering how abrupt had been his departure from them on Bond Street a mere week ago. But expect it she did. After all, a gentleman did not kiss a lady as Marlowe had and then abandon her in a fit of pique. Even if the gentleman was a rakehell. One would think he would be even more likely to pursue the acquaintance in that event. But Marlowe seemed to have lost interest in her completely, and the gossip passed along by her sharp-tongued sister-in-law that he was presently falling at the feet of one of London's more notorious flirts was disheartening. The fact that the lady was older than Gillian and far more experienced didn't ameliorate the situation.

After a day or two of sulking Gillian had developed a sudden passion for Hookham's Library, making at least two visits a day no matter what the weather, but with no success. Madame Racette's had likewise proved a disappointment, as had the parties she had forced herself to attend. They had been dismally dull affairs, and Gillian told herself she should have known that a rackety fellow like Lord Marlowe would never have allowed his elegant person to grace such mundane festivities, but she couldn't help watching for his familiar form. By the end of seven days she was ready to scream from vexation, and it had only been Bertie's ill-disguised look of misery that had penetrated her own wretchedness. But she had provided no help, and only added worry about him to her burdens. With a sigh she went in search of Felicity. She could always be relied upon to brighten a gloomy day.

Felicity, at five o'clock on a spring afternoon, was lying on her bed, a bandage wrapped around her delicate jaw, a lace cap on her curls, and a suspicious flush to her cheeks and a gleam in her dark eyes.

"My dear child!" Gilly exclaimed, stifling her inward pang of despair over one more problem. "Are you feeling unwell? I had no idea."

"I'm afraid I have the toothache," Felicity replied in muffled tones. "Mama has given me some laudanum drops to dull the pain, and I expect I will simply sleep through the night. I do hope you weren't counting on my accompanying you to the Drelincourts' tonight. It should be a dreadful squeeze, and I am certain they won't miss me."

"They won't miss either of us," Gillian said briskly. "I had no real desire to go, and your father will be greatly relieved. He has made it clear these past three days that he cares for the Drelincourts not one bit, and your mama has expressed a preference for a small card party at the Toussaints'. Now they may gladly go, and I will keep you company this evening."

"But I don't need company!" Felicity cried in surprisingly strong tones. "All I desire is a good night's sleep, and I have little doubt I shall feel splendid."

"I have seldom found toothaches to be so accommodating," her aunt observed wryly. "Perhaps I should have a look at it."

"No!" Felicity wailed. "I can't bear to have it mauled about. Please, best of all my aunts, just let me sleep. I am certain you'll have something to keep you occupied, for I shall be no company whatsoever. Have you read Mrs. Overstreet's newest romance?" She gestured to two slim marbled volumes by her bed.

"That trash!" Gillian sniffed, diving for the lurid novel with eager hands. "I don't know how you can bear this romantic drivel. As if any sensible female would behave in such a way, throwing everything away for love. Is it as good as *The Vicar's Revenge?*"

Felicity paled at the unfortunate title. "Even more nonsensically romantic, Gilly. You will adore it."

Gillian looked down at the girl in the bed. "You might have a fever," she suggested worriedly. "Your eyes are bright, and your cheeks are flushed. Perhaps we should call a doctor."

"Please, Gilly!"

"Oh, very well," she sighed. "But you must promise to call me if you feel worse."

"I promise." Felicity pulled herself upright and suddenly threw her arms around her aunt's slender form. "I love you, best of all my aunts."

Gillian returned the embrace with enthusiasm. "And I love you too, widgeon. Feel better soon, please. I need someone to pour my troubled heart out to."

"Tomorrow, Gilly," Felicity promised, and Gilly failed to notice the quickened breathing or rapidly pounding heart of her mischievous niece.

"Tomorrow," she agreed, and retired to her bedroom and the lurid delights of *Virtue Rewarded or the Lady's Conscience*. It was somewhere near midnight when sleep finally claimed her, still in the midst of that exciting tale. For a moment, before she drifted off, she remembered her ailing niece and contemplated checking to see if she was resting comfortably. But she knew from experience that Felicity hated to have anyone fussing over her unless she really felt ill. Either way, she would be better off sleeping the night through without an overprotective aunt sneaking into her bedroom. With a sigh Gillian closed her eyes again and gave her subconscious mind over to the possession of Ronan Marlowe, completely unaware that Felicity Redfern was at that moment making her determined way across the back gardens to Blakely House, Marlowe's family residence.

IN THE MEANTIME Lord Marlowe himself was enjoying a decidedly uncomfortable evening at the gaming salon. First he had had to suffer Vivian's pointed questions concerning the progress of their wager. Questions that had not been soothed with Marlowe's lazy smile and the assurance that things were advancing just as he had envisioned.

"Does that mean she's ready to fall?" Viv demanded as he drained an overlarge glass of brandy. "You haven't been seen with her in a week—been seen hanging about the dashing widow Frenshawe, so I hear."

"Merely a smoke screen, my dear Viv."

"I would have thought things had taken a decided turn for the worse."

"You are unacquainted with my strategy, Viv. I have piqued the lady's curiosity. Rest assured I know precisely what I am doing."

"Ah, but then, I have a thousand pounds that says you do not know what you are doing, Marlowe," his cousin replied, a sly look in his milky blue eyes. "And quarreling with her outside of Hookham's Lending Library is no way to convince me otherwise."

"How news does get around! I am astounded at the number of people interested in my goings-on, Vivian. It truly amazes me." His mouth curved in an amiable smile that failed to reach the hard green eyes, and had Vivian Peacock any sense he would have admitted to a sudden nervous qualm.

Before he could speak a scratching sounded at the door, and one of Marlowe's discreet servants entered the private drawing room that had recently witnessed the beginning of Gillian's downfall. "There is a gentleman who insists on seeing you, my lord."

Marlowe yawned. "Haven't I employed Hobson to take care of difficult gentlemen, Tilden? I would have thought having an ex-boxer for a doorman would have spared me from such embarrassment."

"Throw him out," Peacock ordered casually, pouring himself another glass of brandy and heading toward the door with a slight weave in his gait. "Or damme, I'll do it myself."

Tilden kept his face impassive, the flinty eyes expressing his opinion of the dissolute Mr. Peacock, who hadn't much success with the servant classes. "Hobson said to tell you he would be delighted to do so, sir, but it's not a question of someone who's had a bit too much to drink. It's a minister, sir, and he seems to be in a tearing rage. Says it's personal."

"Throw him out," Vivian said drunkenly. "Give the place a bad name, having the clergy frequent it, don't you know." He subsided in a fit of giggles as he wandered out into the public rooms.

Marlowe sighed. "You'd best show the gentleman in, Tilden. And see if Mr. Peacock might not be persuaded to leave a trifle early tonight."

"It is already past two in the morning, sir," the butler had the temerity to point out.

"Well do I know it," his master sighed once more.

Liam Blackstone scarcely allowed the door to close behind him in the elegant confines of Marlowe's private rooms when he advanced menacingly upon his reluctant host. "What have you done with her?" he demanded, his rich voice shaking with rage. "What have you done with that poor, innocent child?"

Marlowe stared at him for a long moment before rising languidly to his full height, a number of inches over Liam's slender frame, and held out a well-shaped hand. "How do you do?" he inquired smoothly. "I'm Marlowe. And you . . . ?"

"You know damned well who I am," Liam snarled, knocking the politely proffered hand away. "I'm the man whose life you've destroyed."

Marlowe raised an eyebrow. "And how, dear fellow, have I

managed to do that when I've never even met you?" Marlowe inquired civilly.

"I'm Liam Blackstone!" Liam announced accusingly. Marlowe continued to look politely blank. "Miss Redfern's fiancé."

At this point an emotion did cross Marlowe's face, namely rage. "Miss Redfern's fiancé?" he grated out. "She failed to mention your existence to me."

"You failed to ask!" exclaimed Liam. "You were so intent on seducing an innocent girl you didn't even bother to find out whether she might already have given her heart to another."

"Apparently she had," he said ironically. "Is it too much to hope that she hasn't already bestowed other parts of her anatomy upon you?" He avoided Liam's flailing fists quite neatly, controlling his own strong desire to mill down the handsome, wild-eyed boy in front of him with noble restraint. With a dispatch that attested to his prowess at following the fancy and the many hours during which Gentleman Jackson himself had allowed his lordship to pop in a few hits, he bundled the enraged Liam into a chair, shoving him back with a notable enthusiasm every time he leaped forward.

"Stop enacting me these Cheltenham tragedies, I beg you!" Marlowe said witheringly. "I am sorry if you feel I have cut you out in the lady's affections, but I hardly think you should attack me."

"If you mean honestly by her I would take my heartbreak like a man," Liam declaimed nobly. "But to seduce her, entice her to your house . . ."

"Don't be absurd, man!" he snapped. "Miss Redfern has never been in my house. Not that I wouldn't like to get her there, I do admit. But I know better than to attempt such a thing."

"Then why did she send me a note tonight saying she had accepted your invitation for a midnight supper and had renounced all claim to my heart? I never thought she would go so far. I . . . I love her. I only wanted what was best for her. She deserves so much more than I can ever give her."

Marlowe was watching him with a puzzled expression on his dark face. "She certainly does. But as you can see, the hour is far past midnight and Miss Redfern is nowhere around. Nor has she been here for more than a week. You may ask anyone, though I would suggest you not do so. A lady's reputation is at stake."

Liam's beautiful dark eyes clouded with confusion and pain. "But I don't understand. Why would she lie? What would she have to gain?

I . . . I was going to bring a gun with me. I could have killed you, and all over a misunderstanding."

"Why didn't you bring a gun?" Marlowe inquired curiously, pouring two glasses of brandy and handing one to the flustered cleric.

"I . . . I couldn't find one. I am not in the habit of using firearms in the city, you know," Liam said stiffly, trying to refuse the brandy.

"Drink it, damn you." Marlowe's voice was abrupt, his patience at an end. "You need it even more than I do. And then I would like you to answer some questions."

"What sort of questions?" he demanded suspiciously, taking a cautious sip of the brandy and letting out a sigh. It was a very fine brandy, and Liam, despite his monastic tendencies, appreciated a good brandy.

"Concerning Miss Redfern. I think I have the right to ask them, since you seem intent on my giving up any claim I might have toward her. Let me assure you, if I had known she was attached I would never have . . . have . . ."

"Cast your wicked lures in her direction?" Liam supplied furiously, remembering that this soft-spoken gentleman with the lazy smile was his beloved's seducer.

"Well, I doubt I would have phrased it in just that way," Marlowe replied apologetically. "But I suppose that will have to do. I can understand perfectly why she would prefer you to me. You look like the very model for 'The Corsair.' But I wonder if you aren't a trifle young for her."

"I am twenty-six!" he shot back, his face pink from the Byronic allusion.

"Exactly so. And Miss Redfern is thirty."

"Miss Redfern is eighteen!"

Marlowe stared at him for a long, incredulous moment. "Are we discussing Miss *Felicity* Redfern?"

"Of course," Liam snapped. "Who else?"

"I was under the impression it was Miss Gillian Redfern who was the subject of my unholy attentions. For such, I must assure you, is the case. The only thing I would like to do with Miss Felicity Redfern is to spank her."

"Gillian? You mean Felicity's aunt?" Liam was still a few paces behind. "But what would you want with Felicity's aunt?"

"I would suppose precisely what you want with her niece," Marlowe said with a grin.

"Marriage?"

Marlowe shrugged. "I'm afraid not. My intentions are not so honorable as your own, I must confess. Ascribe it to my wickedly sinful nature. You will be pleased to know, Mr. Blackstone, that I have met Miss Felicity Redfern on only two occasions, during which she interfered with my pursuit of her aunt to an annoying degree. I am afraid she is making a may-game of you, my dear boy."

"No doubt you're right." Liam stared at the Aubusson carpet in numb misery. "I know her far too well to deny that such is a distinct possibility."

"I would suggest you go home and get a good night's sleep. I am certain the light of day will bring forth an explanation of Miss Felicity's little stratagems. I have no doubt you could ascribe better motives to it than I could."

"She wants me to marry her, sir," he offered. "And I told her I didn't deserve her, and I couldn't."

"I would think the shoe is on the other foot," Marlowe observed. "In any case she seems determined to prove it."

Liam appeared much struck. "That must be it. I am amazed her aunt let her send that note."

"You may also rest assured that Miss Gillian Redfern would not so forget her responsibilities as to let her niece compromise herself. Trust to it that Miss Felicity is safely asleep in bed. Tomorrow, if I were you, I would go and castigate her soundly, and then agree to marry her."

"Her parents don't approve."

Marlowe snorted. "I would expect I can do something about that also. Go home, Mr. Blackstone, and get some rest."

# Chapter Fourteen

LORD MARLOWE WAS half right. Felicity was sound asleep in bed. Unfortunately, it was his bed.

It hadn't taken a very great deal of ingenuity for Felicity to gain entrance into the fastness of Blakely House on Bruton Street. Both Redfern misses were only too aware that his residence was visible from the third story of Redfern House, and a week's perusal had armed Felicity with the information that the windows of what appeared to be Marlowe's study were usually left open to the damp night air. She was a strong, agile girl, and climbing over the railings and onto the small wrought-iron balcony had proved no more than a mild challenge. It had taken her longer to find Marlowe's bedroom in the dark, deserted stretches of hallway, none of the apartments suiting her notion of what a hardened sybarite would inhabit. But finally she chose the large front suite, not because of its simple, almost Spartan furnishings that hardly brought to mind the rakish Lord Marlowe, but because she recognized his extensive wardrobe in the adjoining dressing room.

As she stepped out of her morocco dancing slippers (a bit damp from her midnight sojourn) she felt a flash of doubt assail her. But Liam would receive her note, she could count on that. And she had it on Bertie's reluctant authority that Marlowe never left the gaming hell on St. James's Street until well into the morning. By that time she would be rescued and well on her way to Gretna Green if she had anything to say about the matter. Thinking of Liam's dangerous eyes and warm, bold mouth, she climbed onto the huge, soft bed with a sigh, burrowing down beneath the coverlet and wriggling her toes. To be sure, it was an obscenely large bed, just the right size for all manner of orgies, but then, Lord Marlowe was a very large man. No doubt he needed all this room to rest in comfort. She wondered what Gillian would think if she were to see it. With a yawn she nestled down farther into the inviting warmth and closed her eyes, prepared to wait in comfort for her rescuer. In a few moments she was asleep. So soundly did she sleep, in fact, that she failed to awake when a tall gentleman strode into the darkened chamber a few hours later, swore under his breath at the sight of her guileless repose, and beat a hasty retreat.

"MISS GILLIAN!" Flossie's piercing whisper finally penetrated through the mists of sleep, and Gillian sat bolt upright in her elegant room on Berkeley Square, her heart pounding in fright.

"Good heavens, Flossie, what's come over you?" she demanded irascibly. "You frightened me half to death. What time is it?"

"Half past four, miss. I'm sorry to waken you, but I wouldn't have except that it was ever so important. I've got a message for you."

"A message for me?" Gillian found herself matching Flossie's whisper. "At four in the morning? Have you lost your senses?"

"No, miss. It's from Lord Marlowe, miss."

All trace of drowsiness vanished in a flash. With shaking hands Gillian lit the tinder beside her bed. The candlelight revealed her flighty maidservant in even greater disarray than usual. With a great effort Gilly forced herself to be calm, swinging her legs from the warmth and comfort of her soft bed. "I think you'd best try to explain this, Flossie, calmly and rationally, if you think you could manage. First of all, how did you manage to get a message from Lord Marlowe at this hour?"

Flossie's ruddy face flushed a deeper shade. "I was visiting a gentleman friend," she stated with a touch of defiance. "Lord Marlowe's head coachman, James, if you must know."

"At four in the morning? Never mind, Flossie. I cannot say that I am surprised."

"Well, it's a fortunate thing I was there, what with the servants tearing all over the place, and his lordship demanding someone sneak into your bedroom and leave you this note," she said with self-righteous dignity.

"He demanded what?" Gilly shrieked.

"If you'll let me finish, miss," Flossie said in an aggrieved tone of voice.

Gilly took a deep breath. "Please continue."

"Miss Felicity is there. At least, that's what James told me in the strictest confidence. He got it from the housekeeper, who knew we were keeping company, but none of the other servants are supposed to know about it."

"Don't be absurd. Felicity is sound asleep with the toothache." Even as she spoke Gillian was assailed with strong misgivings.

"No, she's not, miss. I was so bold as to check on my way in here, and her bed is filled with pillows made to look like she was sound asleep. She's been up to something these past few days, and I don't doubt for a moment that Lord Marlowe is in the midst of it."

Gillian shook off the numb feeling of despair that had swept over her. "You said he sent a message?" Her voice came out sounding surprisingly normal, considering the depths of her misery.

Belatedly Flossie pulled a thick vellum note from her deep cleavage and handed it to her mistress. "He said as how you was to come straight back with me before anyone could find out," she continued, going on in her artless prattle as Gilly read the brief message in the strong, bold handwriting that seemed characteristic of the man.

*Miss Redfern.*

*Your tiresome niece has chosen to involve me in her latest harum-scarum adventure. If you have any feelings of pity for an aging rogue, you will come to my rescue immediately. I've sent for her fiancé, but I have little doubt he may be tempted to run me through when he espies the wretched contretemps Felicity has forced upon me.*

*Marlowe*

"Oh, my heavens," Gilly breathed, aware of a strong feeling of relief washing over her. "That miserable, wretched girl. I warned her she would go too far. Find me some clothing, Flossie. Something simple that I may throw over my night rail. I haven't time to dress properly."

"You aren't going over there, are you, miss?" Flossie asked, scandalized. "To a gentleman's house? At this hour of the night?"

"I most certainly am. I cannot abandon Felicity, even though she richly deserves it. Fetch me that pale blue dress."

"But, miss, that's years out of style . . ."

"Damn you, Flossie, if you won't be silent and do as I tell you I will box your ears. I am in no mood to listen to your chatter," she said abruptly, and then touched the girl's shoulder. "I'm sorry I snapped, Flossie. I'm terribly worried about Miss Felicity."

"That's all right, miss." Flossie sniffed, an irritating habit of hers, as she watched her mistress throw the soft blue walking dress over the thin cotton nightgown. A moment later she protested as her mistress slipped bare feet into a pair of dancing slippers and tossed a light cape around her shoulders. "You're never going out like that, miss!" she protested, horrified. "Your hair all down your back, and scarcely a stitch on under your dress . . ." Her voice trailed off as her mistress turned wrathfully.

"I presume you know how to leave this house without anyone else being aware of it. I cannot believe Letty's housekeeper would countenance your little trysts."

"Yes, miss. But I don't see why you need to be in such a hurry. From the look on his lordship's face I'm sure he wouldn't touch Miss Felicity with a ten-foot pole."

"He wasn't pleased to see her?" Gilly couldn't help but seek confirmation of the note.

"Blazing mad is more like it," Flossie said artlessly.

HE WAS STILL blazing mad when Gillian was shown into his study by a poker-faced butler still correctly attired despite the absurd hour. Flossie was sent to the kitchens to await her mistress, and as the door closed behind Gilly's straight figure she felt a moment's trepidation—trepidation that was not in any way lessened as Marlowe rose from behind the desk, his tall, lean form threatening in the wavering lamplight. His green eyes surveyed her for a long, deliberate moment: the unbound hair a tawny cloud down her back, the thin barrier of clothing feeling suddenly transparent to his slow, languorous regard. Gillian found herself blushing, and Marlowe's eyes lightened as a smile reached them.

"Thank heavens you have come," he said simply, moving across the room in a few grateful strides and taking her unwilling hand in his strong, capable one. "What are we to do with that wretched child?"

"I . . . I don't understand what happened," she stammered, telling herself that he smiled in just that fashion at everybody, that the strong hand holding hers was nothing more to her than a polite gesture.

"As far as I can make it out," he said, drawing her into the room toward the fire and the sofa directly in front of it, "she has concocted some scheme in which she hopes to render herself compromised. She seems to feel that this will make her acceptable to a rather serious young cleric who knocked me up earlier this evening."

"Mr. Blackstone?" Gillian inquired, sinking down on the sofa without recognizing the dangers of Marlowe's proximity. As he nodded, she sighed. "Poor, poor Felicity."

"Poor Felicity?" Marlowe echoed, incensed, as he threw himself down beside her with easy grace. "What about poor, poor Marlowe? If

Derwent Redfern were ever to get wind of it, he would insist I marry the chit. And I have no intention of getting leg-shackled, to her or to anyone else." He spoke the words unflinchingly, and there was no way Gilly could pretend to misunderstand their meaning.

"I don't think that's what Felicity had in mind. Liam Blackstone thinks she's too good for him, and Felicity's parents are inclined to agree."

"They would," Marlowe snorted.

"But she's stayed remarkably constant during the past three years. I think she truly does love him, and I think he would be the making of her. And vice versa."

"Do you? I found them peculiarly ill matched, myself."

"But that's because you've never seen them together. Mr. Blackstone has a tendency to take himself too seriously, and Felicity depresses all his pretensions admirably with a laugh and a turn of phrase. As for her more extravagant habits, he seems able to control them with a gentle reproof. But Letty and Derwent won't be made to see the sense of it. And you see what it leads to? She was ever such a headstrong girl."

"You think they should marry?" Marlowe inquired coolly. "You think that Blackstone might be willing to, after tonight's behavior?"

"You said you saw him earlier. He must know perfectly well that you had no interest in . . . in compromising her." She stumbled slightly over the words.

"No, indeed. He quite upset me for a moment with his rantings and accusations, however." There was a wicked smile on his lean, dark face.

"I wouldn't think it would be pleasant to be accused of harboring evil designs on young ladies," Gilly offered nervously.

"That bothers me not in the slightest. I am more likely to be offended if someone thought I was harmless. No, your Mr. Blackstone upset me with his proprietary attitude because I thought his beloved was the elder Miss Redfern." He was rewarded with an even deeper blush, and his hand reached out to catch one long strand of her silken hair. "I always thought," he continued in a meditative voice, "what a great shame that women are never allowed to have their hair unbound." His other hand came up and caught her willful chin, forcing her to meet his laughing, dangerous eyes. "When it renders them irresistibly beautiful." His voice was husky, and he moved closer, his lips hovering over hers for a long, breathless moment.

"My lord," Gillian breathed helplessly, mesmerized by his proximity.

A smile curved the mouth so very close to hers. "That's rather formal, don't you think?" he questioned softly. "My name is Ronan."

Gillian felt as if she were drowning, impaled by those searing green eyes. "Ronan," she whispered. "Please . . ."

"Don't you think I deserve some sort of reward for the trials and tribulations I have been forced to endure this evening?" His voice was soft, soothing, seductive, and Gillian felt her resolve slipping from her. His mouth was so close, barely inches away, and she could feel his breath warm on her face, feel his heartbeat thudding in time with hers. So very close. It would take but an instant to cross the small barrier that separated them. He was waiting, watching, his eyes hooded, that enticing mouth so damnably close. With a sigh she moved toward him, just as the door to the study was flung open.

The word Marlowe uttered under his breath was in a foreign language, and Gillian could only be glad. Its meaning was far too clear as he jumped away from her, meeting Liam Blackstone's fulminating gaze with surprisingly shaken calm.

"So you were lying to me," Liam began, advancing upon the taller man in a menacing fashion. "I should have known a man of your ilk couldn't be trusted. You low-lying, gutter-crawling, disreputable—"

"Mr. Blackstone!" Gilly rose from her ignominious position on the couch, brushing her trailing hair behind her in an ineffectual gesture. "You owe Lord Marlowe an apology. Felicity has placed him in an extremely embarrassing position, and he doesn't need any more insults from you to add to his burdens."

Liam stared at her, his beautiful brown eyes wide in amazement. "Miss Redfern!" he gasped. "You're here? But why?"

"To try and salvage the harm my niece has done to her reputation, and all for love of you," Gilly said fiercely. "I am surprised at you, Liam. If the two of you had just shown a bit more resolution we wouldn't be in this pickle right now. Don't you realize that Felicity will never be happy with anyone but you? She doesn't care for balls or dresses or society half as much as she cares for you." She was uncomfortably aware of the amusement in Marlowe's hooded eyes as he witnessed this confrontation, but she pressed onward nonetheless. "If you had merely shown you meant to stick by your intentions, my brother and his wife would have acquiesced before long. But you gave in without a fight, leaving my poor Felicity to pine away."

"I hadn't noticed she was pining," Marlowe interjected, and Gilly cast him a fulminating glance.

Liam bowed his head. "I suppose I did give in too easily. But I thought it was God's will that that beautiful creature be denied to me. If I cannot control my wretchedly lustful nature, what good will I be to the people I'm supposed to lead?"

Marlowe's eyes lit up with unholy amusement as he kept his voice grave. "You will be a great deal more help to your parishioners if they know you have human failings as well as they do. Saints are not terribly comforting people, you know."

Liam stared at him in amazement, running a hand through his black mane. "You know, you are absolutely right."

"Of course he is," Gilly broke in. "But the question is now, what are we going to do? Lord Marlowe and I were discussing it when you broke in."

"We were indeed," Marlowe said gently, his eyes playing about Gilly's lips in a tantalizing fashion that made her edge away nervously.

"We'll be married as soon as I can manage it," Liam announced stoutly. "I have no doubt the bishop will help me. He called this morning to inform me that I'm being sent to a new parish. A larger one, out in the country, with a more generous stipend. He thinks the city air is bad for me." Liam appeared unconvinced.

Gillian put a hand on his black-clad arm. "I think the suffering in the city is too much for anyone for long stretches at a time," she said gently. "And I'm glad your bishop recognizes that fact. Felicity will love being in the country, and so will you."

"I must admit I'd prefer it, but will I be doing God's work?" he cried.

"Of course you will," she assured him. "People have problems all over the world, misery and heartbreak and despair. You will be needed there just as surely as you were here."

"If need be the bishop will give me a special license," Liam said, his shoulders straightening as if a heavy burden had been lifted. "Felicity has already turned eighteen—we can manage without her parents' consent if we must."

"I don't think their consent will have to be a consideration." Marlowe's voice startled both of them. "You may rely upon me to see to it."

"Upon you?" Gilly echoed, aghast. "Surely you don't think you'd have any influence in the matter?"

"It may surprise you to know I have a very great deal of influence. Particularly in the case of your esteemed sister-in-law."

"Letty?"

His eyes were alight with amusement. "Letty," he agreed. "A great many years ago she had a fondness for me, one, alas, that your brother did not share. However, I have little doubt I can still exert a trace of influence over her. Especially when the future happiness of her daughter is at stake." He turned to Liam. "My butler will take you to Sleeping Beauty's side. I leave it up to you to break the news to her that not only is she not compromised, but she is going to be well rewarded for her outrageous behavior. I only hope she does not lead you a merry dance, Mr. Blackstone."

"There's no harm in her, sir," Liam said firmly. "It's nothing more than youthful high spirits. Marriage will settle her down."

When he had finally left the room in the butler's impassive wake, Marlowe gave in to the laughter that had come close to overwhelming him during the past few minutes. "I sincerely hope so. Though I doubt anything short of murder will quell that chit's spirits. Why are you staring at me in such surprise, dearest Gilly?"

She ignored the tender appellation. "You? You and Letty?" The notion was as outlandish as it was diverting.

"Why do you think I was banished from my native land?" he rejoined. "I tried to run off with the dear girl. Mind you, at the time she was a mere slip of a thing. I suppose disappointment in love sent her to the chocolate box for forgetfulness."

"How long ago was that?" she questioned suspiciously.

"Twenty years."

"But then . . ."

"That's right. She was also married to your sturdy brother at the time." He smiled down at her with a great show of innocence.

"I am amazed you do not have more feeling for her child then," Gilly snapped. "She might have been your daughter."

"I left twenty years ago, not eighteen," he corrected. "And any daughter of mine would have a great deal more common sense, I do assure you."

"No doubt," Gilly said weakly. "I think perhaps I ought to chaperone the young couple." She began edging toward the door, and Marlowe made no move to stop her.

"I would say, my dear Gilly, that you are in a great deal more need of chaperonage than your idiot niece," he drawled. "You needn't look so terrified. Fetching as you are, dressed so scantily with your hair unbound, I have little doubt that the fire-breathing curate would interrupt us if I allowed myself to forget that I am a gentleman on occasion." He sighed. "I must be on my best behavior."

Gilly just managed to stifle a laugh. "Indeed, you must," she agreed. "We have to set an example for the young people."

Marlowe stared at her for a long, speculative moment. "Damn the young people," he said clearly, and before she could divine his intent he had crossed the room and pulled her into his arms. His mouth came down on hers, effectively banishing the vain hope that it had been the novelty of her first kiss that had so overwhelmed her. The second was even more devastating.

With proprietary hands he molded her body to his, his hands caressing her in a way that should have made her long to slap him but instead had the opposite effect. All the while he kissed her, slowly, lingeringly, thoroughly, as if he had all the time in the world to brand her his possession.

The door was flung open, knocking into their locked figures, and this time Gilly understood perfectly the Anglo-Saxon term Marlowe used. "Come right in, Mr. Blackstone," he said wearily. "I was expecting you."

Liam stood hesitating on the threshold. A very sleepy, shyly happy Felicity stood directly behind him, holding on to his hand as if it were a lifeline. "Felicity wishes to apologize for inconveniencing you, my lord," Liam said formally. "And then we thought we'd best get back to Berkeley Square before the servants rise. That is, if you're ready, Miss Gillian?" Despite a lover's customary preoccupation he belatedly noticed Gillian's flushed complexion and her distinct shortness of breath.

"Perfectly ready," she agreed, skirting out of the way of Marlowe, not entirely sure he might not grab her again. And not entirely sure she might not welcome it. "Good evening, Lord Marlowe. Thank you again for all your assistance."

He smiled his wicked smile down at her. "It was my pleasure," he said, catching her gloveless hand and bringing it to his mouth. It was far from a chaste salute, and Gilly took a deep, involuntary gasp of breath.

And then some daring part of her brought the totally unexpected response. "The pleasure, sir, was mine." Then she ruined the effect by blushing a bright pink before she wrenched her hand away and ran out of the room, leaving Marlowe to stare after his departing guests with a troubled expression in his dark eyes and a reluctant grin on the mouth that had so recently discommoded Miss Gillian Redfern.

# Chapter Fifteen

TO GILLIAN'S MINGLED irritation, relief, and amusement, Marlowe was as good as his word. The very next morning, as she sat hollow-eyed over the breakfast table at the sinfully late hour of eleven o'clock, she overheard a great commotion from the servants. Derwent had just left the house, and scarcely would he have had time to remove himself from sight when the front knocker sounded.

"What is going on, Truffles?" she inquired of the second footman as he raced past the dining room door.

Truffles always had a weakness for the most considerate of the Redfems. "You'll never guess what, miss! Lord Marlowe himself just appeared at the door, asking to speak to Mrs. Redfern alone. I was sure she'd deny herself and send me away with a flea in my ear, but what does she say but, 'Show his lordship right in, and see that I'm not disturbed.' The door closed behind them, and try as I might, I can't hear a thing." He admitted his eavesdropping intent unblushingly, and Gillian took it in the spirit it was intended.

"Did you try the music room door? I believe the wood is a trifler thinner there," she suggested helpfully with just a trace of a smile, trying to stifle her own overwhelming curiosity.

"The first place I tried, miss. They're speaking very low." His youthful face was set in discouraged lines.

"Well, doubtless we'll discover what went on during their tête-à-tête at a later date. Could you bring me more coffee?"

"Certainly, miss." He disappeared in the direction of the kitchens, no doubt delighted with the opportunity to inform the staff what sort of goings-on took place in Mrs. Redfern's drawing room, and Gillian returned to her toast and marmalade with a sigh. The very last person she felt up to seeing this morning was Ronan Marlowe, with his mocking eyes and knowing mouth. A little peace and quiet was all she requested, and the deserted dining room seemed the likeliest place to find it.

She sat there peaceably through the next hour, as she listened to the servants scurrying back and forth, opening and closing the massive front door, ushering visitors into the confines of Letty's drawing room. Truffles remembered her coffee, but from that moment on she was the least of the servants' worries. She recognized Liam Blackstone's beautifully modulated tones in the hallway at one point, and the soft, lazy drawl of Marlowe's counterpoint. Felicity was hastily summoned from her bedroom; Derwent returned home and promptly succumbed to what his undutiful sister could only stigmatize as a temper tantrum before a few well-chosen words from his usually placid and submissive spouse silenced him. When all was finally quiet in the great house, when Marlowe and Blackstone had been dismissed and Felicity had danced upstairs, Gillian rose from the breakfast table with its cold coffee and congealed eggs and strolled into Letty's drawing room.

Derwent and Letty jumped apart guiltily. "Where have you been all morning, Gillian?" he demanded as he shot a quelling glance at his plump wife. "Have you any idea what has been going on here?"

"I would suspect she knows far more than we do," Letty interjected with a trace of venom that was only slightly unexpected. "I am certain it will come as no great shock to you that Felicity is to marry Liam Blackstone."

Gillian schooled her features in an expression of polite surprise, wondering how in the world Marlowe had managed to pull it off. "That is delightful. I've always felt they were extremely well suited."

"I don't doubt we have your interference to thank for this," Derwent harrumphed, not as resigned to the arrangements as his help-mate appeared to be. Letty leaned back with a sigh and popped a chocolate in her small, satisfied mouth.

Gillian decided to ignore her brother's carping. "And when will the great event take place?"

"Three weeks' time," he replied heavily. "The announcement has been sent to the papers. Your sister-in—law will need your assistance with all this unseemly haste. There are invitations to be addressed, a trousseau to be ordered. But don't think, Gillian, that because Lord Marlowe insinuated himself into our affairs this time that he will receive an invitation. It will be a small family affair. Lord Marlowe will have no place there."

Gilly cast a questioning glance at Letty and was disappointed to see her nod in reluctant agreement. "It certainly wouldn't do to pursue *that* connection," she said with a trace of regret in her smug voice.

"But why such haste? When you felt Felicity was far too young to be wed?" Gillian's demon prompted her to inquire.

"It was scarcely my idea," Derwent cried petulantly. "Mr. Blackstone has been transferred to a largish village in Sussex and is to take up his duties within the month. The young people wish to have time to get settled into the parsonage before that time."

"But how delightful!" Gilly clapped her hands together delightedly. "And Felicity has always been fond of Sussex. I couldn't be happier for her."

"Well, I certainly could!" Derwent snapped. "We are all to attend the Belvoirs' rout this evening, with Bertie and Mr. Blackstone accompanying us. You may inform your nephew of the plan, and tell him I will brook no denial. We must present a united front on occasions such as these."

"The Belvoirs?" Gilly made a face.

"Don't try to wriggle out of it, my girl. You may find them dead bores, but there ain't a more proper family in all of London right now. A word here and there, this evening, and the thing will be done right. It will come as no great shock to anyone when the papers print their announcement tomorrow."

"I suppose we must all make some sacrifice to ensure Felicity's future happiness," Gilly said with a mischievous grin.

Her brother was not disposed to be amused. "You may very well laugh," he said sternly, "but it's that care-for-nothing Marlowe who's to blame for it. You can thank him for upsetting all our plans for my eldest daughter!" His voice was bitter.

Gilly smiled sweetly. "That's exactly what I intended to do," she replied.

DERWENT HAD NOT exaggerated. The Belvoirs were, without question, the stuffiest, most proper, most unimaginative, boring, tedious, unspeakably perfect family in all of London. It was, therefore, with a sense of surprise verging on shock that she recognized Ronan Patrick Blakely, Lord Marlowe, across the crowded dance floor, and met his quizzical gaze with a delight she couldn't quite hide.

It had been an excessively tiresome evening. Liam and Felicity had spent the entire time staring at each other, with scarcely a sensible word coming from the pair of them. Letty, placid as ever, was far too lazy to waste her energies in conversation, and Derwent was far too furious. Even Bertie, usually the most charming of companions, was in the worried silence that had become habitual with him in the last week or so, his face pale, his eyes dark and hollowed. It was, therefore, left up to

Gilly to endeavor to entertain herself, aided not very ably by the proper widowers and aging bachelors who were considered suitable dancing partners for a lady firmly on the shelf. Their number was not great, their skill in dancing likewise limited, and not a one managed to penetrate the abstraction that had clouded her mind all evening. She danced the regulation two dances with each of them, all quadrilles and country dances, and then settled herself with the appearance of amiability to watch the waltzing.

"You don't care for dancing, Miss Redfern?" Marlowe had taken no time at all in reaching her side, a circumstance Gilly couldn't help but find gratifying, even if she told herself she must deplore the singular nature of it.

"I am too old to waltz," she replied with a provocative smile.

"Nonsense!" In front of her family's scandalized eyes he pulled her unresisting body to her feet. "You are precisely the right age for me." And he swept her onto the dance floor before she could utter another protest.

It took her a few moments to accustom herself to the novel sensation of being held in a gentleman's arms as she danced. To be sure, she had been instructed in the waltz when it became all the rage three years earlier, but up until now she had only danced with a graceless Bertie or other females also learning the dance. Never had she dared to waltz in public, and the presence of Marlowe, his starched white shirt front a few inches from her face, was not likely to add to her peace of mind. Indeed, as he guided her effortlessly around the dance floor, she felt more as if she were floating, and it was with a real effort that she forced herself to make conversation, when all she really wanted to do was close her eyes and dream.

"How in the world did you receive an invitation to the Belvoirs'?" she inquired artlessly, and then blushed. "I beg your pardon, I should never have asked you such a thing."

"One of the things I adore most about you, Gilly-flower," he said in his low, caressing voice, "is the delightful way you blush. I was invited to the Belvoirs' because I acceded to the title and have not caused an open scandal in the last fifteen years. It is an amazing thing how many doors are opened to one if one has a title and a reasonable sum of money."

"Derwent has asked me to thank you for your assistance in arranging Felicity's future," Gilly murmured.

He raised an eyebrow. "I am certain that is not exactly how he phrased it," he remarked.

"Perhaps not exactly," she agreed. "But he did give you full credit. As I must. I cannot thank you enough for all you have done."

"I had begun to doubt how pleased you were. You were nowhere to be seen this morning, and I had been hoping for a chance to pursue our acquaintance under Derwent's disapproving eye."

"You didn't ask for me." She betrayed her interest and blushed again. "Besides, I would have said our acquaintance has been pursued to quite indecent lengths."

He threw back his head and laughed, causing not a small number of guests to stare at the couple and whisper in disapproving tones. "My dear child, you don't know the meaning of the word indecent. I would be glad to demonstrate."

"No, thank you," she returned politely. "My vocabulary is broad enough."

"Will you have supper with me?" It was nearing time for the midnight buffet, and Gilly felt a treacherous longing.

"I am afraid I couldn't, my lord," she murmured. "Derwent has decreed that the family must present a united front in the face of our incipient disgrace in allying ourselves with one of Mr. Blackstone's humble origins."

"Humble origins? His uncle is the earl of Walston!"

Gilly smiled. "Yes, but that scarcely compares with the Redferns. Or so Derwent insists."

"It is a fortunate thing that my intentions are not honorable," he said lightly. "I can see that Derwent would soon send someone of my paltry heritage to the right-about."

That was the second time in twenty-four hours he had mentioned that he had no interest in marriage. When he returned her to her family, she watched him saunter off with a sharp pain somewhere beneath her ribs that she told herself was too much lobster pâté. Indeed, the manner in which she picked at the dinner Bertie had provided for her convinced her far-from-observant family that she was feeling not quite the thing, and she was immediately inundated with offers to escort her home from the desperately bored Bertie. Letty contented herself with recommending a dosage of Hemenway's Essence of Mandrake Root, which she insisted was just the thing for costive disorders. It was with a great effort that Gilly controlled the strong desire to snap at the both of them and burst into tears. Declining their suggestions gracefully, she took another forkful of cheese custard.

The dancing had already commenced when the Redferns returned en masse to the ballroom. It was nearing the end of a country dance, and Gillian watched Marlowe's graceful figure as he bent over a very pretty young girl scarcely out of the schoolroom, as she told herself bitterly.

Derwent edged over to her, a dark look in his beady eyes. "I do not wish you to dance with Marlowe again," he uttered in tones that would brook no denial. "He is not at all the thing."

The dance was ending at that moment, and Marlowe looked about him with a casual air, having relinquished his ravishing partner to her protective mother. His dark green eyes took in Gilly's angry expression, and Derwent's disapproving stance, and without hesitation he moved toward them, his deliberate, elegant grace reminding a fanciful Gilly of a panther stalking his prey. For a moment she felt very much like a quivering, helpless rabbit under his watchful eyes.

"Miss Redfern, may I have the honor of this dance?" There was a glint of laughter in his dark eyes.

"Gillian!" Derwent warned.

"I would love it." More fool she, she thought as she allowed herself to be swept back into his arms for a second waltz. This entire business of waltzing was far too disturbing to the senses.

"I gather I may thank Derwent for the pleasure of this dance," he murmured. "Did he order you not to stand up with me?"

"What would you expect?" she countered.

He smiled down at her tenderly. "Who would have thought I would find cause to be grateful to Derwent Redfern?" he mused. "I rather thought you might refuse if I asked you again, but I can tell you don't like to be ordered about by a cod's head such as your brother."

To her dismay, Gillian giggled. "I used to let him order me about at will," she confessed. "I think you are having a deleterious effect on my conduct, my lord."

"Ronan," he corrected softly.

"My lord," she replied firmly.

She was obliged to listen to a thundering scold from her livid brother when Marlowe once more returned her to her family's bosom. Even Letty was eyeing her with a look that bordered on jealousy, as her husband kept up a steady harangue.

"Where's Bertie?" Gilly interrupted him suddenly.

"Bertie? He's somewhere about, moping, no doubt. What has that got to do with your outrageous behavior, Gillian?" Derwent demanded.

"I am disturbed about him, Derwent," she confessed.

"And I am disturbed about you! Bertie has been a model of propriety, despite his fatal addiction to gaming, compared to you, miss!" He continued on in that vein for a bit, while Gillian, with a look of dutiful and contrite attention, busily pursued her own thoughts.

Doubtless it was the gaming that had given Bertie that desperate, haggard expression. And not the gaming per se, but the debts that losing incurred. She had little doubt that if luck had smiled upon him he would have continued his normally sunny-tempered self.

He had refused to confide in her, and it was idiotically unfair. She had more than enough money to assist him. Indeed, her personal fortune was a great deal more than genteel, it was positively vulgar, and she had nothing to do with it but spend it on her family. If only he weren't so mutton-headed as to refuse her assistance. And how to offer it if she had no idea of the extent of his losses?

Her eyes lit upon Marlowe's figure across the room Except for his one dance with the ravishing young lady who had turned out to be his second cousin (Felicity had roused herself from her love-struck daze to impart that information to a determinedly casual Gillian), he had remained on the sidelines, his attention apparently absorbed in conversation, except for the occasional mocking glances he would send in her direction whenever he felt her eyes upon him. Which was far too often.

The question was, Gilly thought, moving away from the fulminating Derwent and seating herself by the French doors, how to manage a few words with him? He would know better than anyone the extent of Bertie's debts, or if he was unaware of their full extent, he could certainly find out for her. If only she had thought of it earlier. She had already danced her allotted two dances with him. To dance a third dance with a gentleman was unthinkable, even if one were approached by a gentleman who so forgot himself as to ask. Better to ride stark naked down St. James's Street like a latter-day Lady Godiva than dance three times with a gentleman unrelated to one. There was little she could do that would put her more completely beyond the pale, and even a rakeshame such as Ronan Marlowe would never sink to such a level as to ask her for a third time.

A tall shadow moved in front of her, and she raised her head to meet Marlowe's cool expression. "It is another waltz, Gilly," he observed coolly. "I think I must ask you to dance with me."

She drew in her breath sharply. "We've already danced twice."

"I have not consumed so much brandy that I am unaware of that fact. Indeed, I doubt I would ever forget how many times I have held you in my arms. Will you dance with me?"

"I cannot!" She looked up at him pleadingly. "Indeed, had something of a particular nature to ask you. About Bertie. Could you perhaps procure me a glass of orgeat and we could sit here and discuss it?"

No answering smile lit the dark planes of his face. "As a gentleman I should of course acquiesce. But I am rag-mannered at best, and I wish to dance."

"Then find another partner," she said desperately, her large eyes miserable.

"I don't wish another partner. I wish to dance with you. Have you become so cow-hearted recently? To be terrorized by an idiotish society?"

"There are certain rules of polite behavior . . ."

"Rubbish! I hadn't thought so poorly of you, Miss Redfern." No longer Gilly, she noted mournfully, and his eyes were stern.

"I am afraid I must refuse your kind offer, my lord," she said with as much dignity as she could muster.

"You disappoint me greatly, Miss Redfern. And not just in the matter of the dance. I hadn't noticed a resemblance between you and your brother until tonight." He turned to leave her, his head averted so she couldn't see the amusement in his dark eyes.

"I am not like my brother!" she cried, outraged. He turned back, and his face was expressionless.

"Then dance with me. Show these gossiping old tabbies how little you care for their silly little rules, and I will tell you everything you wish to know about your green nephew." There was a teasing note in his voice that she couldn't miss, one that should have stiffened her resolve. Instead it melted it completely.

She held out her hand to him, hearing Letty's outraged gasp behind her. "You, my lord, are a devil," she said roundly as she followed him out on the dance floor. Every eye in the Belvoirs' flower-bedecked ballroom was upon them, and whispers nearly drowned out the strains of the waltz as he drew her into his arms, a little closer this time.

"And you, my love, are a blue-eyed witch," he whispered, and swung her into the dance.

# Chapter Sixteen

"THERE CERTAINLY was a rare dust-up tonight," Bertie offered as he escorted his shameless aunt up the broad front steps of the Berkeley Square mansion. "Did you really dance with Lord Marlowe three times?"

"I did," Gilly confirmed. "And if Derwent hadn't threatened to create a scene I doubtless would have danced with him a fourth or even fifth time."

"But he hasn't . . . that is to say, he didn't . . . ?" Bertie floundered. "You aren't going to . . . ?"

"I'm not going to what?" Gilly encouraged him, still turning over the sum Marlowe had whispered in her ear. Nine thousand pounds was a very great deal of money to owe, to be sure. But not worth Bertie's complete misery.

"Well, when people dance together more than twice in one evening it usually signifies that they have come to some sort of understanding." Bertie brought it out finally.

"We have. We understand each other, Lord Marlowe and I, and we have agreed to be friends. Nothing more."

"Well, no wonder Uncle Derwent was furious!" Bertie said, much impressed. "You certainly have become brave in the last few weeks, Gilly. I remember a time when you would be in an absolute quake over what Uncle Derwent would have to say about the most minor peccadilloes. And now you commit a major breach of conduct and don't even turn a hair."

"It's scarcely worth all the bother," she said as she handed her cape to a curious Truffles.

"If you say so," her companion said negligently. "If you'll excuse me, Gilly, I think I'll—"

"I most certainly won't excuse you!" She caught his arm. "I am far too wound up to sleep right now, and I need some company. Indulge your poor aunt in a glass of claret and a hand or two of piquet."

"I don't really feel like gambling," Bertie said somberly.

"I rejoice to hear it. I have little doubt you've spent far too much time in that occupation than is good for you. However, gaming at Lord Marlowe's salon and keeping me company are two very different things. I'll get the cards while you have Truffles bring us some of Derwent's best claret and meet me in the upstairs sitting room. I don't expect we'll see the rest of them for several hours yet, and I mean to keep awake long enough to ring a peal over Derwent for bundling me off in such a high-handed manner."

It didn't take her long to arrange the furniture to her satisfaction in the small, cozy salon that usually served the female members of the Redfern family. Truffles stoked up the fire, taking the damp chill off the lofty proportions, and Gillian had him place the baize-covered gaming table in the strategic location she had already discovered earlier. A chair was placed opposite her for her hapless nephew, directly in front of the gilt mirror. The moment he picked up his first hand and settled back Gillian found the reflection in the mirror, and she smiled, well-satisfied with her machinations.

It was not that Bertie was such a good card player. As a matter of fact, his talent at cards was so execrable that Gilly couldn't rely on her skill alone to achieve her aims. Without the aid of the mirror she could play her absolute worst and still Bertie might manage to lose.

"A pound a point, Bertie?" she inquired in dulcet tones, shuffling the cards with a practiced hand.

Bertie took a sip from his claret, not his first glass of the evening by any means, and nodded. "Whatever you say, Auntie," he agreed in a lighthearted manner that convinced Gilly he thought she was simply funning. He would soon find out otherwise.

Bertie's first few hands were played with a throwaway air, as if humoring an elderly relative. As he began to win, however, his attention sharpened, and it took all of Gilly's skill to avoid the obvious mistakes that riddled his playing. If he always played so badly it was no wonder he was in debt. The only wonder was that he didn't owe more.

Marlowe had looked down at her in amused surprise when she had made her request during their final, shameless waltz. "How much does your nephew owe? What a very odd question, Gilly-flower, to be sure."

"He is terribly worried about his debts, my lord, and I wish to help him," she said earnestly, fighting the temptation to snuggle closer to him as he whirled her around the dance floor.

"And you think I am likely to dun him? A fine opinion you have of me, I must say."

"You think Bertie is likely to shab off?" she countered. "A fine opinion you have of my family, my lord."

"I have no intention of telling you anything unless you desist with that stuffy 'my lord.' Sounds like my old nurse when she's angry with me."

"Ronan, would you please find out how much Bertie owes around town?" she questioned sweetly, then ruined the effect by adding, "There, does that suit you?"

"Admirably. And I happen to know exactly how much the hapless Mr. Talmadge owes. Vivian brought up the matter a few days ago." A troubled expression briefly shadowed his eyes. "Nine thousand pounds, and he owes it to me."

Gillian sustained the shock admirably. "A large sum," she remarked, "but not quite as great as I feared. But are you certain? He frequented other gaming hells before yours."

"I believe he had a run of luck just before Vivian brought him to St. James's Street. It must have been extraordinary, for I don't hesitate to tell you, my dear Gillian, that he plays abominably badly."

"You haven't been asking him for the money, have you?" she inquired anxiously.

"If I weren't madly in love with you, Gilly," he said in a mocking tone of voice, "I would pour champagne on your head for that question."

She shouldn't refine on that remark too much, she told herself as she sat across from Bertie. Marlowe had been teasing her, as he always did.

She was distracted enough to accidentally win that hand, and Bertie's face fell.

"I should have known the dibs would never stay in tune," he mourned. "It happens this way every time—I have a short run of luck and then it peters out. Peacock always tells me my luck will change, but it never seems to."

"Well, you're already fifteen hundred pounds ahead of me, Bertie," Gillian pointed out. "And the night is still young. I don't see what you have to complain about."

"Fifteen hundred pounds," Bertie giggled, good humor restored. "Ha, ha. That's good, Gilly."

"Good indeed," she said serenely, and dealt the next hand.

He ended up by winning nine thousand, six hundred pounds, Gillian having decided that he needed a new hack and doubting his purse-pinched father would stand the ready. The last of the claret was gone, and Gilly leaned back in the comfortable chair, well pleased with her night's work.

"I'll tell you something, Gilly," Bertie confided owlishly as he drained his glass. "I don't think I really care for gaming all that much."

"Don't you? I am relieved to hear it. It certainly isn't a very comfortable addiction."

"As I was winning all I could think of was why it should matter. Tell you what, I don't think I really have the brain power for it."

Gilly smiled. "I think everyone flies a great deal too high for you in London. If you care to gamble with a few friends for small stakes on occasion, I see nothing wrong with it, but it truly is a fatal addiction." She covered her mouth with one slim hand as she yawned daintily. "I'll give you a draft on my bank tomorrow, Bertie. For the money I owe you."

He stared at her, momentarily sobered. "What money?"

"The nine thousand, six hundred pounds I just lost to you," she replied demurely.

"Don't be absurd!" Bertie cried. "I thought you were in jest. I hadn't realized we were really playing for that sum of money!"

"Hadn't you? Then it is fortunate that you are the more expert player," she said mendaciously.

"But I can't accept the money from you. It just isn't done!"

"Bertie"—Gilly's voice was stern—"are you telling me that you refuse to allow me to discharge a debt of honor? How dare you suggest that I have less scruples than the most ramshackle gentleman."

"No, I didn't mean to say that, Gilly," he replied desperately. "But can't you see, I cannot accept all that money from you."

"No, you can't accept it," she agreed. "Not as a gift. But you can and must accept your winnings. You beat me fairly, and I will pay you. After all, I was the one who set the stakes."

"But you cannot afford it!"

Gillian smiled. "Don't be absurd. I would never play for more than I could afford to lose. Ninety-six hundred pounds will never be noticed. My money merely sits in the bank and makes more money. Derwent refuses to allow me to spend any on my upkeep, so I have to fritter it away on gewgaws and gaming and various other profligacies."

A faint ray of hope was forming in the back of Bertie's usually desperate eyes. "Gilly," he breathed, "must I accept the money?"

"You must."

He let out a long, shaky breath. "Very well, if you insist," he said finally. "I know just what I'll do with it, too."

"More gaming, Bertie?" she inquired, holding her breath.

He shook his head. "Absolutely not. Better to end my gambling career in a blaze of glory. I have, a few trifling debts"—here he had the grace to blush—"to discharge, and then I think I might possibly buy a new horse. That is, if you approve?" he added anxiously.

"It is your money, my boy, won fairly," she replied. "You may do with it as you please. Though I must say such a program sounds admirable."

"And, Gilly," Bertie added hesitantly, "you really ought to be careful."

"How do you mean?" she returned warily, expecting a homily on the dangers of Lord Marlowe.

"You shouldn't play for such high stakes when you play so very badly. If you like I might give you a few pointers on piquet sometime," he offered in a kindly tone.

Gillian kept a straight face with a great deal of effort. "That is sweet of you, Bertie, but I think I might follow your lead. Gaming seems far more trouble than the momentary thrill it offers. I would—did you hear something?" Voices were reaching Gilly's sharp ears from the front hallway.

"They must have returned."

"Then I'm off to bed. I suddenly feel quite unable to face Derwent in all his disapproving glory this evening. Meet me tomorrow in the breakfast room at eleven, and I'll give you a draft."

"Are you quite certain . . . ?"

"Bertie, the more you protest the more you offend me," she warned, heading for the door.

"I wouldn't want to offend you for the world, best of all my aunts," Bertie swore, and then leaned back in his chair, a seraphic expression on his face, as Gilly happily stole off to bed.

# Chapter Seventeen

GILLIAN SPENT A languorous morning. She rose quite late, as was to be expected from a lady who retired a few minutes before daybreak. She had a solitary breakfast in her small, elegant room at Berkeley Square consisting of croissants, fresh fruit, and coffee, a Gallic fest the rest of the family highly disapproved of. That morning she was in no mood to listen to their everlasting criticism.

An hour at her small, papier-mâché desk was similarly felicitous. Several missives of a nature that would have startled the majority of the Redfern family were penned, along with a bank draft for nine thousand six hundred pounds for Bertie. And there was money well spent, she thought, pushing away from the desk with a satisfied smile and stripping off her frilly lawn dressing gown. Ninety-six hundred pounds in return for a sweet-natured young man who had faced temptation and would no longer be captured by it was a bargain at the price. She had no doubt that Bertie would be able to resist the lure of gaming from then on. And his friends, young Porter and Willie Meekham were far more addicted to sport than the lure of the dice. No, he would be fine.

And so would Felicity, she thought, dressing slowly in a round gown of soft rose wool. Her happiness fairly seemed to permeate the darkest corners of the Redfern house, and even Derwent had been seen to smile on occasion last evening, before Gillian had fallen from grace with such a resounding thud. Now it only remained, she thought wistfully, to manage her own life as well as Felicity had.

"Miss!" Flossie exclaimed from the doorway. "You've gone and dressed yourself, and without even calling me."

"I wanted to be alone, Flossie," she replied distantly, strolling toward the windows that overlooked the square, one hand twirling a tawny lock lazily. "I am certain you have been busy enough."

"Yes, miss. Would you like me to fix your hair?"

"No, don't bother," she said, peering with her excellent eyesight at the passersby down below on the street. "I don't intend to do much more than read today, and I don't require anything . . ." Her eyes narrowed, and her voice trailed off as a familiar figure strolled into view. She waited one more moment to make certain the Redfern house was his destination, and then flew to the dressing table. "Don't just stand there, Flossie," she cried. "Help me with my hair."

Like most less-than-needle-witted girls, Flossie grew clumsy and even slower under pressure. She pulled Gilly's hair, dropped the hairbrush three times, and burst into tears when Gilly finally grabbed the pins from her servant's useless fingers and did it herself. There wasn't time for the usual severe style, and the hair was falling in loose waves about her face as she raced down the flights of stairs to the drawing room. It wasn't until she reached the tightly shut door that she realized she wore neither stockings nor shoes.

Only for a moment did she consider racing back to her rooms for those essential accessories. Abruptly she put it out of her mind, bending her knees slightly so her wool skirts would trail along the fortunately dust-free parquet flooring, and doing her best to glide gracefully into the drawing room—a feat that is extremely difficult when one is in a semicrouch.

Derwent and Letty were sitting alone, their heads together in a fashion that was decidedly suspicious. No stretch of the imagination could encompass the thought of romance between the ill-suited couple, so Gillian could only assume they were plotting. Of Lord Marlowe's tall, saturnine figure there was not a trace.

"Yes, Gillian?" Derwent inquired frostily.

"But . . . where is Lord Marlowe?" she demanded, remembering to keep her knees bent. If Derwent were to espy her bare feet she would be back in Winchester before the sun set.

"Why should you expect that reprobate to be here?" he queried icily. "After last night—"

"But I saw him," Gilly interrupted. "I was looking out the window, and I saw him head straight for this house."

"Then common sense should tell you that he has been denied," Letty broke in sharply. "We don't want his sort making themselves free of our home. And we certainly don't wish to encourage his attentions toward you. They are scarcely honorable. If they had been, it would have been Derwent he wished to speak to this morning, not you."

"He wanted to see me?" she shrieked, outraged. "And you denied me?"

"He did indeed," Derwent nodded, a cool, superior smirk on his face. "With the message that Miss Redfern does not wish to see his lordship again."

Gillian's cornflower-blue eyes widened in rage and despair. "Damn you!" she cried, and ran from the room before Letty could collapse in a dead faint.

Truffles was standing by the door. "Miss Gillian," he hissed as she stormed out of the room.

She stared up at him, a question in her tear-filled eyes. "I had to give him their message, miss," he said apologetically. "They were standing right there listening. But I managed to wink a few times, and I think he understood. At least, I do hope so."

Hope sprang in her breast. "How long ago was this?"

"Why just half a mo' before you came downstairs. He's not even at the end of the square yet."

Gilly reached up and gave the young footman a resounding kiss on his angular cheek, a cheek that turned bright red. "Bless you, Truffles," she cried, and reached for the door.

"You're never going after him, miss!" he breathed, scandalized.

"I most certainly am."

"But it's cold out there. Let me at least get you a wrap and come with you."

Remembering her bare feet, Gillian crouched once more. "Not that cold. I'll be back in a few minutes, Truffles. See if you can sneak me back in with no one noticing?" And she was off, her bare feet racing over the marble steps.

Fortunately the square was fairly deserted. It was a trifle early for morning visits, and late for the day's deliveries. Marlowe was a fair bit ahead of her. Lifting up her skirts and exposing her bare feet, she took off after him at a dead run.

When she thought he was in hearing, she dropped the skirts, settling into a running crouch, and called his name. "Marlowe!"

If he heard her he made no sign of it, the broad back continuing on at a casual pace, swinging an ebony cane. "Marlowe!" she cried in a louder voice, and still he failed to check. "Ronan!" she tried, and as if by magic he stopped, turning toward her with a lazy smile.

"I thought you didn't wish to see me again, Miss Redfern," he said coolly as she reached him.

"You know perfectly well Derwent sent that message, not I!" she cried hotly, her feet icy on the chill pavement.

"Normally I would have thought so," he agreed. "But I received a visit from young Talmadge this morning. He informed me that he would pay all the money he owed me later this afternoon. Apparently he won it from his aunt. Vivian has told me many times how bad a player your nephew is, and I can only assume you cheated so he would be able to pay me. A lady who assumes I would dun green youngsters would hardly wish to pursue the acquaintance." His eyes were chill with anger in the morning sunlight, at odd variance with the mocking smile on his mouth.

"Don't be absurd!" she cried. "I did it for Bertie's sake. He would have been mortified if you had let the debt drop. *I* knew perfectly well that you wouldn't press him, but I couldn't very well tell him that."

The rigidity in Marlowe's face relaxed slightly. "That is a point," he conceded.

"Then you aren't angry with me?" she asked anxiously, her toes numb.

He surveyed her for a long moment, and the green eyes began to warm. "Perhaps just a trifle. You must find some way to placate me, dear Gilly-flower."

"And how would I do that?" She was conscious of a feeling of excitement warring with the panic in her breast.

"You must finish what we started on your birthday." His smile was definitely wicked.

"What!"

"The game of piquet and dinner, dear one," he soothed. "Nothing more, nothing less. You are safe with me."

"I'm sure that I am," she agreed with a flash of self-deprecating humor. "If seduction was on your mind you could do a great deal better."

If Gilly hadn't known better, she would have said it was anger that flashed across Marlowe's dark face. "We can discuss that this evening," he said smoothly, his face shuttered.

"This evening? I don't know whether I can manage to escape . . ."

"You, my dear Gilly, can manage anything you set your heart on, I have no doubt. In the meantime, don't you think you'd best get back to your house? You'll likely catch inflammation of the lungs and expire before this evening if you don't, and I have no intention of letting you escape so easily." He smiled his sweet smile that had the unfortunate tendency to make Gillian's heart turn flip-flops. "I'm greatly flattered that you thought it so urgent to come after me, but perhaps next time you might remember your shoes." They both stared downward at the delicate bare feet just peeping out from under Gillian's hemline.

She blushed a deep, mortifying red and crouched down again. "Shall I send my carriage for you?" he continued suavely, watching her blush with amusement.

"No, I would prefer to get there on my own," she said in a strangled voice. "What time would you like me?

"If I were to answer that honestly you wouldn't approve, so I shall say whenever you can safely escape from your relatives," he replied. "I have little doubt they'd disapprove heartily."

"I don't see that I need to tell them."

He reached out a hand and brushed a stray lock from her flushed face. "Hoyden," he remarked appreciatively. "Shall I escort you back?""

"Not if you value my life. Till this evening," she promised recklessly, and took off, her bare feet flying over the chill pavement. When she reached the Redfern portal she allowed herself one brief glimpse backward as Truffles tried to pull her inside. Marlowe was still standing there, watching after her. It was too far away to see his expression. On impulse, Gilly waved her hand. She had just enough time to see him return her lighthearted salute before Truffles forcibly dragged her into the deserted hallway, shutting the heavy oak door behind her with silent care.

Gilly leaned against the door, her eyes shining, cheeks flushed from cold, feet half frozen, a dazed smile on her face. "Truffles," she said in a dreamy voice.

"Yes, miss?"

"I am in love," she sighed. "In love, in love, in love."

"Yes, miss." A shy smile lit his face. "I'm very happy for you, miss."

"And so am I, Truffles," she murmured dazedly. "So am I." Humming an aimless little tune, she wandered up the stairs, her hand trailing along the banister, her feet doing a careless little dance on the carpeted stairs. "In love, in love, in love." Her voice floated down into the empty hallway on a soft sigh, and then she was out of sight.

# Chapter Eighteen

GILLIAN SURVEYED herself in the dim candlelight of her bedroom. It was going on ten, and the house was deserted except for the servants. The entire Redfern family, accompanied by Felicity's beaming fiancé and a strangely lighthearted Bertie Talmadge, had departed hours earlier for a ball at the Castlereaghs', and Gillian, having pleaded a headache, knew she could rest assured that her absence wouldn't be noticed if, by some strange chance, she happened to arrive home after the Redferns.

She truly hadn't thought that far ahead. As she eyed her reflection approvingly, she didn't stop to think what effect the décolletage of the clinging silk gown would have on Marlowe. Her hand strayed toward the bit of lace she customarily used to preserve her modesty, then resolutely withdrew it. Her tawny hair was a cascade of artless ringlets down her back, artless ringlets that had taken her hours to achieve. She had even been prepared to use paint to enhance nature, but in the end there had been no need. No need for belladonna drops to put a sparkle in her eyes, no need for red papers to put a flush on her pale cheeks or color to her tremulous mouth. In the dim light she looked seventeen years old, and in truth, she felt it.

"This is madness," she told herself frankly. "You must be out of your mind." She reached for her thin cloak and draped it around her nearly nude shoulders, drawing the hood protectively over her head, giving herself one last, anxious glance in the mirror before securing her reticule.

"Are you ready, miss?" Flossie, her brainless accomplice, hissed from the doorway. "The coach is waiting." She peered through the gloom at her usually staid mistress. "Are you certain you wish to do this, miss?"

Gillian snuffed out the candle on her dressing table and gave one last look around the room. "Absolutely certain," she said, and the waver in her voice was not noticed by her maid. Touching the diamond earbobs that swung from her shell-like ears for luck, she swept from the room.

WHEN SHE STEPPED from the carriage she stared about her in dismay. "This isn't the front entrance, Truffles," she informed the second footman, dragooned into service for the night.

"I was told to bring you to this doorway, miss," he said, gesturing toward the entrance with his whip. As if in answer, the door opened, and a staid, reserved-looking manservant appeared. "Miss Redfern?" he inquired in sepulchral tones. At her nod he continued smoothly onward. "His lordship thought it might be better if you were to use this entrance. A bit more discreet. You may leave, coachman. His lordship will see Miss Redfern home."

Truffles stood his ground. "Are you certain you want to stay, Miss?" he inquired with a trace of belligerence.

Gilly was half tempted to run back to the safety of the carriage. The hallway just inside the door was bright and well lit, and the butler beside her looked so very proper that she should laugh at her misgivings.

"There's no need, Truffles," she replied in a deceptively steady voice. "I am certain I can trust Lord Marlowe to take care of me."

An undutiful snort was all the answer Truffles offered before moving away. With strong doubts about her own sanity she watched the small, closed carriage disappear down the rain-swept London street.

"This way, miss." The servant beside her gestured, and she had no choice but to enter.

"Is this the way all his lordship's lady friends visit him?" she inquired, only half facetiously, as she picked her way up the winding stair, her cloak held tightly around her. Why had she worn such a low-cut dress, she thought with a belated trace of desperation. She was practically naked underneath!

"Not usually, miss," he replied, leaving her as uninformed as before. At the top of the stairway was a small landing, a hallway, and at the end, a doorway. The man beside her moved ahead, opened the door, and announced her in the same gloomy tone of voice.

She stepped inside and found herself directly beside the gold-draped bed at the far end of the room from Marlowe's amused gaze. With all the coolness at her disposal, she averted her eyes from that embarrassing piece of furniture and moved toward her host with head raised and shoulders back.

With his usual lazy grace he came to meet her. "You look as if you're on your way to the guillotine," he greeted her quizzically. "Very brave, very noble, and very beautiful. I'm not going to eat you, you know."

Gilly's shoulders relaxed their militant pose, and she allowed a small smile to escape her firm lips. "I trust not," she replied. "You promised me lobster at least."

There was a fire blazing in the hearth by the sofa; the heat penetrated Gilly's chilled bones. She hadn't chosen her clothing for warmth that evening, and with a small shiver she pulled the protective cloak closer about her.

"I can tell by that gesture that it would be useless to try to take your wrap. May I interest you in a glass of champagne and a seat closer to the fire?"

"Champagne?" she echoed suspiciously, taking the seat proffered. It was the sofa, but she remembered hazily from her previous visit that that had been a surprisingly safe perch.

Not tonight. Marlowe lounged beside her, his long legs stretched out in front. "You could always drink brandy," he suggested affably. "It would warm you up in no time and take some of that panic away from you."

"Panic?" she echoed in an outraged squeak. "I am hardly afraid of you." That last came out in a slight waver that belied her strong words, and she expected Marlowe to laugh. Instead, however, he put a gentle hand up and pulled the hood from her head, smiling at her in a way that was far more disturbing because it contained none of his usual mockery.

"Of course you're not," he agreed. "And why should you be? I'm a fairly harmless gentleman, when all is said and done." His hands moved to the ribbons at her neck, untying them deftly before she realized what he was doing. She reached up her hands to stop him, and his strong, warm grasp caught hers, and held it. His dark green eyes met hers for a long, searching moment, and her breathing grew rapid under his gaze.

"I don't for a moment believe that," she said, and her voice was husky.

The hand released hers, and he rose abruptly, striding across the room toward the far doorway. "I'm having Tilden wait upon us tonight," he said with a carelessness that was belied by the tension in his broad shoulders. "I've locked the door to the gaming salon and told everyone I'm not to be disturbed. I thought it would be better if no one knew you were here."

"Doubtless," she agreed nervously. "They must be somewhat used to this."

"Hardly. But I have little doubt Vivian will contrive to muddle through without my assistance." He strolled back toward her, pausing to refill his brandy glass but making no attempt to pour one for her.

"He, of course, is in your confidence."

"He, least of all," Marlowe said enigmatically, coming to stand above her while he swirled the brandy in his glass. "Aren't you going to take off that wretched cloak?"

"It isn't a wretched cloak. It's my very best one," she said, stalling for time.

"Well, then, aren't you going to take off that very attractive cloak?" he inquired, the mockery back.

Taking a deep breath, Gillian pushed the wrap off her shoulders, keeping her eyes downcast. It was the prettiest dress she had ever worn, and she sat there, waiting for some slight expression of appreciation. There was dead silence. Finally she raised her eyes and looked at Marlowe.

He was staring at her with an odd expression on his face. "You look . . . very nice," he said finally.

She couldn't understand the strange undercurrent in his voice. "You don't like it?" she asked doubtfully.

"Oh, I like it very much. Far too much, as a matter of fact," he said grimly, draining the half-full brandy glass. "Tell me, Gilly, why did you come here?"

"Because you asked me to," she replied, at a loss.

"And would you do anything I asked you to?" he demanded. "Don't you realize that if anyone knew you were here you'd be ruined?"

"I realize it," she said quietly.

"And you realize that I have never once mentioned marriage as any kind of possibility? And that I never will?"

"Yes."

"Then why are you here? Why aren't you home safe in your virginal bed, safe from rakehells like me?" There was real pain in his face as he towered over her, and Gilly longed to reach up and smooth away that expression, the cause of which she couldn't even begin to guess. Unless, of course, it was put there by a sudden, latent surge of guilt. The thought was as unlikely as it was curiously touching, and Gillian dropped her last defense.

"Because I love you," she said quite simply.

"You *what?*"

"I love you," she repeated patiently. "You asked me to come, and I did."

"And would you get into that bed with me if I asked you to? Knowing I won't marry you?" he demanded harshly.

"Yes."

With an explosive oath he rose, stalking across the room. "Where the hell is Tilden?" he demanded of no one in particular. He turned back to the astonished Gillian. "Put your cloak back on. Tilden is taking you home. Now."

"But I don't wish to go home," she said in bewilderment, not moving. "You promised me a lobster dinner and a hand of piquet."

"Among other things," he agreed bitterly, taking her wrists and pulling her to her feet. "Well, I've thought better of it. You're going home before any more harm is done, and no one will be any the worse for it."

"But I want to stay here with you!" she cried. "You took Letty, why not me? You've never lied to me, you know. I thought . . . I thought that you found me not unattractive. Don't you want me?" The tears that had been hovering in her bright blue eyes spilled over and ran down her pale cheeks, and with a curse Marlowe pulled her into his arms.

"Dear God, of course I want you," he murmured into her hair. "I've never wanted anyone so much in my life. And it's because of that that I'm sending you away. I don't want to ruin your life as well as my own."

"If you send me away you'll ruin my life," she said, and reaching up, she put her mouth on his.

He was unyielding, his mouth like marble, and she started to draw back, stricken, when he suddenly yanked her to him, cradling her head in one large hand, and took over the kiss.

It was . . . astonishing. His other kisses had aroused her, excited her, twisted her with longing. This was something entirely different, so much more powerful than anything she could have imagined. He tipped her head back, slanted his mouth across her, and pushed her mouth open with his, shocking her with the feel of his tongue. She jerked, startled, but he held her tighter, sliding his arm around her waist, drawing her up against him as he kissed her. She wanted this. She didn't care what he did with her, she wanted whatever he would give her, for as long as it could last, and she put her arms around his neck, rising up into his kiss, using her own tongue in shy imitation of his.

He groaned and lifted her so that she fit more closely to him. He was much stronger than she had realized, and she could feel the insistent push of that part of him she wasn't supposed to know existed, pressing against her skirts, and another frightened thrill sliced through her veins as she held on, letting him do what he wanted, wanting more. She was wicked, wanton, and she didn't care.

And then to her horror he set her back on the floor, trying to pull away. "You need to get out of here, Gilly-flower," he said hoarsely. "You're not this kind of woman."

She didn't release her hold on him. "I want to be. I've spent my whole life doing just as I ought, taking care of everyone else. I want tonight. Just for once, I want something for me."

"Oh, Christ," he muttered under his breath. Before she could realize what he was planning he'd scooped her up in his arms and was carrying her toward the shadowy back of the room, to the ornate bed that she'd dreamed about, setting her down on the soft mattress and then stepping back.

"Should I . . . should I undress?" Gilly asked, wishing there wasn't a slight quaver in her voice.

He didn't move. "Is there any way I can get rid of you?" he asked in a harsh voice, and it felt like a knife to the heart.

She moved fast, rolling to the far side of the bed and leaping off it, trying to keep the sting of tears from her eyes. She stood still, staring at him across the rumpled bed. "Don't be absurd, Lord Marlowe," she said with a brittle laugh. "I certainly didn't mean to importune you. I'll leave." She started moving away from the bed, away from him, when he caught her.

"No, you won't. Damn me for a selfish, rutting bastard, but I can't let you go." He pulled her against him, and she struggled, just slightly, until she realized her dress had come loose and was sagging about her shoulders. He'd somehow managed to unlace the complicated thing with the deftness of a master. This time when he loosened his hold her dress fell away from her, pooling on the floor, and she stood in front of him in her stays and shift, frozen.

He was just as adept with the corset, stripping it off and then lifting her onto the bed clad only in her shift. He reached for her foot, taking off her kidskin dancing slipper and tossing it to one side, then removing the other, leaving the stocking that were tied to her thighs in place. "Lie back," he said in a low voice.

Automatically she did what he told her. "Do I get to keep this on?" she asked, hopefully.

His smile was slow, wicked, as he shook his head. "I just want to enjoy taking them off you."

He slid his jacket from his shoulders with an ease that belied its excellent tailoring, tossing it to the floor so that it settled on top of her discarded gown, following with his waistcoat and shoes. He pulled his shirt free from his pantaloons, and then he stripped it off, leaving her face to face with the first male chest she had seen without clothing, and she took in a breath.

He was beautiful. There was no other word for it. He had broad shoulders, muscled arms, and oh, my heavens he had hair on his chest. Just a small amount in the middle that led down his stomach to disappear into his waistband, and she stared at him in shock.

"You have hair!" she said stupidly, wanting to touch it. Would it be rough, or soft? But she shouldn't touch him—he was the one who was supposed to do the touching, wasn't he?

"What an innocent you are," he said with a soft laugh. "Haven't you ever seen a man without a shirt before?"

"Farm workers," she said. "From a distance. I didn't realize . . ." She'd never seen the outline of hair on the Greek statues she'd studied so assiduously when she thought no one would notice. Apart from that he seemed to be built along similar, beautiful lines. And then she remembered that other part of the statues that had held her attention, which clearly differed from Marlowe's body.

He reached for fastenings of his trousers, and she couldn't help it, she closed her eyes. She heard his soft laugh, and the mattress dipped beneath his weight. His mouth closed over hers, and her fear vanished. All she needed was the warmth of his skin against hers and she had no doubt.

He pulled her down, beneath him, as his mouth brushed against her skin, her eyelids, cheekbones, back across her lips as one hand tangled in her hair, managing to divest her of hairpins with the same economy of motion.

"You must have a lot of practice at this," she said, trying to sound normal beneath the hitching of her breath.

"You'll thank me for that later," he whispered, moving his mouth to her ear, breathing against it, and then to her shock, he bit into her earlobe, and a shiver arched through her body.

He moved down, slowly, his warm, damp breath warming her through the tissue-thin shift, and she needed to hold onto something. She tried to dig her hands into the linen sheets, but even in the shadows he must have had a preternatural sense of what she was doing, because he caught her wrists and placed her hands on his shoulders. His warm, bare shoulders.

"If you want to hold onto something you should hold onto me," he whispered And then he touched her breasts, not gently, cupping them, rubbing against the center until she felt herself harden against him, felt the warmth of longing curl deep in her belly, and she was panting, tilting her head back, and closing her eyes. The sensation was exquisite, strong and delicate at the same time, and she was restless, needing more, not sure what she needed.

Until his mouth covered one breast through the thin batiste, wet and hot and seeking, his tongue rubbing against the hardened nub, and she let out a helpless little moan.

"You like that, Gilly-flower?" he murmured. "That's good, because I like it, too." He blew on the damp cloth that covered her breast, and she shivered in reaction. He caught the loose neckline of her shift, and before she realized what he was doing he'd ripped it in half, down to the hemline, pushing it away from her body, and then his mouth was on her skin, and he was sucking at one breast while his fingers plucked the other.

He was kneeling between her legs, and she realized with mixed relief and regret that he still had his britches on. Would they stay on? Probably not, not if she was going to be naked.

"You have perfect breasts," he breathed against her. "Just right for my mouth." He licked at her other breast before taking it into his mouth, and she arched her back slightly, searching for something she couldn't define. His arms slid beneath her, and he rolled her across the bed, so that she lay facing him, with no choice but to meet his eyes, dark with desire. Desire for her. He took one of her hands from his shoulder and brought it to the center of his chest, letting it rest against the soft crinkle of hair. His nipples were hard, too, and she wondered if she was supposed to lick him as well.

"I . . . I don't know what I'm supposed to do," she said haltingly.

Again that devastating smile, devoid of his usual mockery. "You just have to lie back and enjoy yourself. This is your night. But you're going to have to get used to things." He covered her hand with his, and moved it down his chest, his warm, flat belly, to his breeches, and then he placed it against that un-statue-like bulge, and it was bigger than before. It was huge, a rod of iron beneath his pants, and she shivered in sudden fear.

"Are you going to hurt me?" she whispered, unable to hide her trepidation.

He slid her hand up and down his shaft, a slow, sensuous caress that seemed to have the unfortunate result of making him even harder, bigger.

"A little bit, I'm afraid," he said. "I'm told it always hurts the first time, but I plan to make up for that."

"All . . . right," she agreed, still game but slightly doubtful. She'd felt pain before—she'd broken her leg falling from her horse when she was thirteen, and it had hurt like the dickens, and she'd once accidentally cut herself on a gardening tool and needed the cut sewed up like a ripped piece of fabric. She'd survived that. She could survive this.

She let her fingers wrap around him beneath the material, and his eyes glazed slightly as he let out a soft curse. She immediately yanked her hand back. "Did I hurt you?"

His laugh was unsteady. "No. But for some reason my usual iron control seems to have abandoned me, and I want to make certain you reach pleasure before I come."

She almost asked him what he meant, but shyness stopped her. She would understand it when he was done with her. He would hold her and kiss her, and they would talk. That's what her mother said made the whole messy business bearable, but she wasn't sure she trusted her mother. She wanted more than cuddlings and kisses. She wanted his body taking hers, changing hers, whether it was for this night or for longer. He would forget, but she would always know she belonged to him. She had told him she loved him, and she wasn't the kind of person who loved easily. He'd warned her, and she had no illusions.

He was watching her. "What are you thinking about?"

"My mother."

He rolled onto his back with a weak laugh. "Good God, that's the most ghastly thing I've ever heard."

"My mother told me this was messy and unpleasant, but that I'd like the holding part afterwards. But I'm not sure she was right. Because if the holding part was the part that mattered, why do the other thing?"

He moved back, pushing her down on the mattress, the light of amusement still in his eyes. "Your mother was wrong. Oh, it's messy, and undignified, and wet . . ."

"Wet?" she interrupted in confusion.

"Definitely wet," he purred. "And if you do it right you no longer have any control over your body."

She frowned. "I'm always in control."

"Not tonight. Not when I make you come."

There was that word again. "What do you mean, 'come'?" she said.

"I'll show you." He moved over her, blotting out the dim light, and she had the sudden feeling she was past the point of no return. Then again, she'd reached that point when she'd stepped into her carriage that night.

He was so big, looming over her, that it should have frightened her, and nervousness danced across her skin, but stronger still was the desire to reach up to him, to be absorbed by him, sinking into him so that there was nothing left of her.

She could feel his hand moving across her skin, sure and deft in the darkness, slightly calloused, not like the soft hands of the gentlemen she had danced with, not like her uncle or cousin Bertie. His touch was like nothing she'd ever felt, and she gave a soft whimper of pleasure as he moved over her stomach. Down, down, until he slid between her legs, and she jerked in shock.

"What . . ?" she stammered. "That's not what you're supposed to do!"

"Who's the expert at this?" he said in a low, beguiling voice. "You're just lucky I don't go use my mouth this time. It's something I particularly like, but I've decided you're in for enough surprises already."

Use his mouth? He was using his mouth, sucking at her breasts with deliciously animal intent. That couldn't be right either, but it had felt so wonderful she hadn't objected. This part of her, that he was touching, was another matter.

"Stop worrying," he whispered, brushing his lips across hers, and his fingers slid through the embarrassing dampness between her legs, moving the moisture around and around until she found her body arching against the mattress.

"That's right," he murmured softly, and she felt him push a finger inside her, stretching her, sliding through the wetness, doing what he would soon do with the rest of his body. It was strange, uncomfortable, but she had wanted this, and when he pushed two fingers inside her she made a shocked noise.

"This isn't going to work," she gasped, and he laughed softly.

"It always does." He touched her, the pad of his thumb pressing, rubbing, and she cried out at the sudden, electrifying sensation.

His too long hair almost hid his face in the shadows, and he pressed his mouth against her cheek as he continued the slow, deliberate rubbing against her, all the while he kept moving his fingers, stretching her.

It was strange, unsettling, and she squirmed, pushing her feet against the mattress as her body grew hot, and then cold, and then strangely hotter still, and her skin began to prickle. "I don't . . ." she gasped.

"You do," he said, and she exploded, lost in sensation, frozen, trembling, crying out until he pulled her against him, pushing her face against his warm shoulder to quiet her sobs.

He held her for a long time as slowly, slowly her soul began to return to her body. She was still shaking, and she knew her face was wet with tears, but she simply burrowed closer to him, hiding, as he held her, stroked her, whispered soft, inconsequential words in her ear full of love and praise. "That's my sweet darling," he said, kissing her tear damp cheek. "You'll survive."

She wasn't quite certain of that, or even if she wanted to, but she took his word for it. She lay tucked up against him, limp with reaction, unable to move, to talk, and she heard his soft laugh. "And that, my love is what it means to come."

She tried to say something, but nothing came out. When it finally did all she could manage was a weak "oh, my."

He pushed her onto her back, and she looked up at him as he loomed over her, moving between her legs. She could feel his skin against her thighs, and she knew he'd discarded his breeches at some point though she had no idea when. She considered looking down, then thought she'd better not. This entire endeavor seemed fraught with difficulties already, and she was better off not knowing.

He moved over her, his eyes glittering in the darkness, his hand between her legs again, and her sensitive flesh jumped. "My turn, Gilly-flower," he whispered. "I'll try not to hurt you."

She could hardly protest, not after the astonishing thing he had done for her, so she braced herself, closing her eyes tight, waiting for the pain.

He didn't move. "Open your eyes, love."

She didn't want to, but when he called her "love" she would do anything for him, on the slight, unlikely chance that he meant it. "Relax," he said, "or I may have to tickle you."

For some reason that made her laugh, and her body loosened. It was no longer his hand between her legs, but that part of him, hard and blunt, pushing against her, and for a moment she froze, then made her muscles relax once more, as he pushed inside her, slowly, slowly. She wanted to close her eyes again, so he wouldn't see her distress, but she couldn't look away from him despite the burning sensation. His hands were bracing his body above hers, and she reached out to hold his arms, hold on to him, as he slowly forced his way into her body. She was prepared for the ghastly part, the horrible, impossible part, but when he was finally, fully inside her, his body against her, the man-part inside her, she knew she'd survive.

He held very still, but she could feel his arms were like iron, trembling slightly as he fought for control. "Did I hurt you?"

She was feeling oddly emotional, but she strove for calm. "It's not as bad as a broken leg," she said judiciously.

He laughed, and she felt it deep inside her, the oddest sensation, and she felt her body begin to relax around his invading one. The burning feeling was fading fast, replaced by something else.

"Do you want to continue?"

She knew how much it cost him to ask her that. Knew that if she said no he would withdraw, stop what he was doing. And if he stopped, she would die. "Yes, please," she said politely.

With something between a groan and a laugh he put his forehead against hers, and then he kissed her, so sweetly that she wanted to cry. "Then hold on to me," he said, and began to move.

At first she told herself she could survive this, easily, and she tried to will herself to relax. The discomfort began to recede and she felt her body begin to move, instinctively, to arch up against his, and when she did the pleasure began again, those powerful, frightening sensations that had overwhelmed her earlier. What had seemed impossible before was becoming glorious, filling her, taking her, claiming her, and when he reached down and pulled her legs up around his lean hips a sizzle of heat shot through her, and she cried out.

He somehow knew he no longer hurt her. He kissed her as he thrust inside her, his face almost brutal in the firelight, and she put her arms around his neck, holding him against her, the crisp hair on his chest rubbing against her breasts, the feel of him so powerful she wanted to cry out in pleasure. She could hear the slap of their sweat-damp bodies coming together, could feel the slide of his skin against hers. He was moving faster now, hammering into her, and she took him greedily, wanting more, the word coming from her mouth. "More," she whispered brokenly, and he gave it to her, and she knew she was going to do that mysterious thing again, that she was going to come, and this time she wasn't sure she would survive.

He reared up and slid his hands between their bodies, to the place where they were joined, and he touched her, hard, and this time there was no muffling her cry. She felt him pull free from her, and she reached out with desperate hands to pull him back, but he collapsed on top of her as warm, wet liquid jetted across her stomach. A moment later he pulled his heavy weight off her, collapsing beside her, and he lay on his back, his breath fast, one arm over his eyes.

Gillian's own response had slowed, and she watched him in the darkness as he struggled to regain control. She felt strangely mournful, bereft, and she didn't know why. Perhaps she was supposed to get up now, go home, but she wasn't sure her legs would hold her quite yet. Her mother said the holding was the best part, which she took leave to doubt, but that was between husband and wife, not between illicit lovers, which is what they were. Or perhaps they weren't, if this was the only time they'd be together, if he'd taken what he wanted and had lost interest in her. She could hardly compete with the experienced women he usually bedded, and her mother had assured her that men were only interested in conquest, and perhaps she should . . .

"Come here, widgeon." His soft voice came out of the darkness, and he hauled her up against his slick body, wrapping her in his arms. She felt all her dark thoughts leave her as she sighed and curled up against him, oddly, mournfully happy.

"You think too much," he said in her ear, pushing back her tousled hair.

"I know," she confessed meekly.

"Was that better than a broken leg?"

Her own laugh sounded rusty to her ears. "Much, much better." He was stroking her, calming her, and she wanted to arch like a cat beneath his hard, caressing hands.

"Was your mother right?" he asked her sleepily.

"Well, it was messy," she said. "And undignified."

"And wet," he prompted.

She could feel the wetness between her legs, on her stomach, the sweat, the tears. "Very wet," she agreed. "I like wet." And then she asked the question that had been plaguing her. "But why did you pull away from me, at the end?"

She could feel a momentary tension in his body. "To keep you from getting pregnant."

"Oh." She wasn't sure what she thought about that. She hadn't even considered what could come from this night, and suddenly she wanted his baby inside her, something she could claim forever when he dismissed her, which might be in a few hours.

She burrowed her face against his chest. She wouldn't think about that. She would be happy for now, at least. She would face the eventual desolation when it came. She wanted to stay awake while he slept, to lie in his arms and drink in the sensations, hold them to her, but she was drained, limp, exhausted.

"So are we going to do this again?" His voice was so soft she almost didn't hear it. "Or was tonight enough for you?"

A warm joy blossomed in her heart. "One night isn't nearly enough," she whispered, pushing herself up to place a soft kiss on his mouth. A lifetime wasn't nearly enough, but she'd take what she could get.

"Then go to sleep, Gilly-flower," he said, brushing her hair away from her face and tucking her against him. "We'll deal with things in the morning."

What things? she thought sleepily. What was there to deal with? But she wasn't going to worry about that now, with his heat all around her. For now she was just going to let go and love him.

GILLIAN DREAMED as she slept in his arms. She dreamed of a happy life in the country, of chasing around her own children and not someone else's, children who looked like Marlowe. She dreamed of lying in bed with him, night after night, of exploring all the astonishing things they could do with their bodies. She dreamed they had spaniels running at their heels as they walked on the grounds. She dreamed the door opened, and someone was coming toward them in the dark. Someone was looming over them, and Marlowe's body stiffened, instantly awake, and she knew it wasn't a dream, it was disaster.

"Well, well, how extremely edifying." A voice broke in, and Gilly jerked up, the covers pulled up high to cover her breasts, only to face Vivian Peacock. He was standing beside the bed, a key in one hand and a scrap of paper in the other.

"What the bloody hell are you doing here?" Marlowe demanded furiously, moving to shield her from Vivian's gaze, but it was already too late.

"Why, you know perfectly well what I'm doing here, old man," Vivian said in a voice that was silken with menace despite the drunken slur, his pale little eyes bright with malice. "My spies tell me that you've finally managed to compromise Miss Redfern. I felt it behooved me to check on the proof. I don't want to lose a thousand pounds without being absolutely certain."

"A thousand pounds?" Gilly echoed, suddenly very cold despite the blankets she'd pulled around her.

Vivian granted her a swift leer as he swaggered around the bed toward her, the scrap of paper outstretched. "You might be interested to know, Miss Redfern, that all this comes out of a wager between Ronan and me. I bet him he couldn't compromise you before the end of the season. Bet him a thousand pounds, too. I never thought Derwent Redfern's sister would sink so low. But he was right, damn him. Always are, aren't you, Ronan, old boy? You could seduce a nun without even trying. Perhaps that should be our next wager."

Gillian ignored the paper, turning her pleading eyes to the silent Marlowe. "He's lying, isn't he?" she begged. "You wouldn't have done anything so cruel?"

"Yes, Ronan. Tell her I'm lying," Vivian said affably, a vicious smile wreathing his cherub's face. "If you can make her believe that you can make her believe anything. But I wouldn't count on getting too much from her. I have another little present for you, due to arrive tonight."

"You really do hate me, don't you, Viv?" Marlowe observed with an air of wonder, beginning to climb out of the bed.

"I always have," he spat out the words. "Whenever you were around no one would look twice at me. Even when they sent you away they said at least you had some spirit. Not like poor, foolish Vivian. You've even thrown a rub in my attempts to wring a little bit of money from the green young gentlemen who frequent this place, a place I designed, a place that should in all rights be mine! But I think I can feel suitably revenged for all those years of living in your shadow. The young lady is waiting for your answer."

Marlowe turned to Gillian's accusing gaze, his face impassive. "It's true," he said briefly.

Gilly stared at him for one long, heartbroken moment. The first time she'd seen him fully nude, and a numb part of her still responded to his fallen angel beauty. She turned away, scrambling out of bed, dragging the blanket with her. Her shift was in ruins, her clothes were on the floor beneath Marlowe's, but she had no choice. She came around the bed, pushing past Vivian, and caught hold of her dress and discarded slippers, determined not to look up at Marlowe standing just above her.

In one direction lay the gaming rooms, and she could hear the noise and chatter. She had to move past him to leave the way she'd come. She could dress in the hallway, escape down the stairs, and flag a hackney. Or she could walk, and inebriated gentlemen would think she was a street whore. They wouldn't be far from wrong.

"That explains a great deal," she said in a deceptively even voice. "I'll leave you then, Lord Marlowe. I believe we've concluded our business."

She started for the door, and he put out a hand to stop her, but she jerked away. "Don't," she said in a very dangerous voice.

In the next moment she was gone.

# Chapter Nineteen

"EXCUSE ME, MY dear. I wonder if you could help me?" A heavily accented voice, accompanied by a strong waft of perfume, made itself known at her elbow, and she whirled around in surprise.

She had been surveying the dark, early-morning streets of London outside the back of Marlowe's gaming salon, desperate to find a hired carriage to take her back to Berkeley Square. Her emotions were held in check, on a very tight rein, but more than anything she wanted to be alone in her room where she could scream and weep and throw things and curse herself for a perfect fool.

In the lamplight the lady next to her at first appeared to be strikingly beautiful. Her large brown eyes dominated a heart-shaped face, her midnight hair was an artful crown of ringlets, and the full-blown figure would have appealed to more than one man's appetite. The clothes were elegant, if a bit overly so, red satin being a bit bright for formal wear. As Gillian peered closer she noticed the tiny lines radiating from those pretty eyes, and the neck added another decade to her years. A mature beauty, not even in her second youth. She put her mittened hand beseechingly on Gillian's arm, and yet Gilly felt that this was a woman who seldom failed to get precisely what she wanted. She wanted to yank her arm away, just as she had with Marlowe, but she was a lady, or had been until tonight, and she knew how to hide her strong emotions with a proper exterior.

"How may I help you, madame?" she inquired politely, pushing her misery back farther.

"I was wondering if this truly is the residence of Lord Marlowe?" she inquired prettily. "My coachman insists that it is, but I can scarcely credit it. I would have thought Ronan would be living in the highest kick of elegance."

Gillian stared at her, wanting to throw up. Finally she answered. "This is his gaming salon, madame. His residence is on Bruton Street."

"And where is his lordship right now, eh?" she inquired. "I can tell by the miserable expression on your face that Ronan has been up to his old tricks. Has he broken your heart?"

"Not likely," Gillian replied stiffly. "And yes, his lordship is upstairs. I am sure anyone can direct you to him."

"I wonder . . . could you be so kind as to escort me?" The lady begged prettily. "I do hate wandering around unfamiliar places. And after you do, my coachman will be pleased to drive you wherever you wish. Which I hope, for such a pretty young lady, is to your home."

Gillian shook her head. "I'm afraid I cannot. You are extremely kind, madame . . ."

"Actually, I am Lady Marlowe," the foreign beauty said with a small preen. "But you must call me Helene."

The numbness was spreading, chilling Gillian's heart and reaching over her entire body. "You are Lord Marlowe's wife?"

"Indeed, yes. I haven't seen my dear Ronan in almost three years, so I was delighted when Vivian's letter reached me. Not that I have any intention of dancing to *his* tune," she confided. "Please, my dear."

Gillian was too numb to stop her as the woman pulled her through the front doors of the gaming palace. She wanted to pull away, to run, but Ronan's wife had a grip on her arm that was almost unbreakable, and the last thing she wanted to do was make a scene.

"I had reasons of my own for seeing my husband again, reasons I have no doubt he'll be glad to hear," Lady Marlowe said confidingly. "Especially now that I've met you, Miss . . ."

"Redfern," Gilly supplied in a fog. "I am Gillian Redfern."

"And Ronan no doubt calls you Gilly," she said shrewdly. "You aren't at all in his usual style, *chérie*. He tends to confine his attentions to the older, more experienced sort."

She was turning to a block of ice. "I believe I was more in the nature of a wager," she replied, as Marlowe's wife pulled her through the crowded salon. More than a few pairs of eyes watched their passing, and the level of conversation sank to a furtive whisper.

Without bothering to knock, Gilly reached out and opened the door to Marlowe's private rooms, gesturing her ladyship to enter. Helene did so in a manner that suited a duchess better than a countess, and Gillian knew she should leave, but a cold rage had settled over her, and she followed Marlowe's wife, closing the door behind them all and turning to survey the scene.

It was a surprising tableau. Vivian was lying on the floor, his nose bleeding furiously and one eye closed. From the moans and groans it was apparent that he was still conscious, but preferred his position of comparative safety on Marlowe's Aubusson carpet.

Marlowe himself was staring at Helene with mingled disbelief and exasperation. His knuckles were grazed, no doubt from contact with Vivian's unyielding nose, and the lines around his mouth were grim.

"*Chéri!*" Helene cried, holding out her scented arms to him. He eyed her coolly, ignoring Gillian's waiting figure.

"What are you doing here, Helene?" he said in a cool voice.

"Your charming friend Gillian brought me up here. Aren't you happy to see me, *mon amour?*" Her full red lips curved into a pout that was meant to entice.

Marlowe remained stonily unmoved, his green eyes hard as emeralds as they flitted briefly over Gillian's still figure before they returned to his wife's opulent form. "Not particularly," he said. "And I meant what brought you to England?"

"Actually, it was your friend Vivian. Or may I assume that the two of you are no longer friends? Very wise, I must say. He is far from trustworthy."

"Thank you for your advice, Helene," he said ironically.

"I have some more advice, *chéri*. I can tell that you have treated Miss Redfern very badly. You didn't used to be maladroit with the opposite sex. You must apologize to her for ill using her so, and—"

"Will you mind your own damned business!" Marlowe exploded.

Vivian chose that moment to try to sit up, apparently secure in the knowledge that Marlowe wouldn't harm him further with two witnesses. "Helene?" he murmured piteously, peering up toward her out of one rapidly closing eye.

"Yes, my dear, it is me," she replied briskly, moving toward him and helping him to rise to unsteady feet. "All your plans have gone awry, have they not? Poor little cabbage. I could have told you that you shouldn't cross swords with my dear husband. Come along with me, and I'll clean you up a bit. You do have other rooms, do you not?" she inquired of Marlowe, who gestured roughly to the left. It wasn't until the two unlikely companions were out of the room that he allowed his brooding gaze to fall on Gillian.

She came to with a start. "Good evening, Lord Marlowe," she said hastily, starting for the door. He was there before her, reaching behind her head to hold it shut.

"Will you give me a chance to explain?" he questioned in a low, bleak voice.

"What is there to explain?" she shot, determined not to react to his nearness, shocked that she still did. "You admitted to the wager. Are you going to deny it now?"

"No."

"Then what do you want?" she cried. "Haven't you enjoyed yourself enough at my expense? Surely you don't need to torment me further."

His mouth moved a fraction of an inch closer, and she could feel the heat from his body as it held her prisoner, a few inches away from her, the door hard at her back.

"Gillian," he said softly, urgently. "I never meant this to happen. I merely thought I'd give you a taste for some of the things you've been missing, cooped up as a slave to your relatives, never having a life of your own. I thought I would show you what life is like, and then you could find someone suitable and marry him. I didn't mean to hurt you so badly, just to . . . to bruise you a bit."

"How devastatingly kind of you," she said with heavy sweetness. "So all this was done purely out of noble motives? I should have known. Haven't I always insisted you were much maligned? And even I hadn't guessed the depths of your philanthropy. Such an effort you've been making, and so selfless of you! Of course, there was the thousand pounds besides, but I'm certain that was of little moment to you. Did you ever think of joining the church, my lord? With your selfless nature I have little doubt you'd make sainthood in a matter of months."

"Gilly, don't!"

"What is needed now, my lord, is an apology," she continued, her cornflower-blue eyes bright with rage and unshed tears. "Just to clear your conscience, of course, and to make me feel truly wretched. Come now, it's very simple. Just say, "My dear Miss Redfern, I am sorry for any inconvenience I have cost you, and deeply regret leading you on like this." And then I will say very prettily, 'Oh, no, your lordship, it is perfectly all right,' and we may part civilly."

"I'm not sorry."

"What?" Her voice rose to a modified shriek of fury.

"I said I'm not sorry," he shot back, biting off the words. "I'm only sorry I was too much of a gentleman not to carry you off to the Continent and be damned to society."

"And to your wife?" she inquired in icy tones. "You haven't changed much since you tried to elope with my sister-in-law. Adultery has always been a part of your life, hasn't it? And did it amuse you to make me fall in love with you? It must have had you roaring with laughter at the thought."

"You will be well pleased to know, Gillian, that you have already had your revenge," he said quietly.

She stared up into his compelling eyes. "I rejoice to hear it. And how have I managed that?"

"By making me fall in love with you." The words were small and quiet in the suddenly still room, and Gilly stood stock still.

"You . . . you bastard!" she hissed finally, shoving him away with all her strength. "How dare you say such a thing? Liar! Cheat!" Before she could scream at him further her struggling body was pulled into his arms, and his mouth came down, silencing her tirade.

It was a kiss of passion and desperation, of longing and farewell. Gillian, her senses playing her false, responded to it, all the time cursing herself for a fool, but knowing it would be the last time. When he finally moved away, she reached out and slapped him across the face with all her might.

The sound of it was shocking in the silent room. The two combatants stared at one another, both breathing heavily, both pale, with the mark of Gilly's hand showing red on Marlowe's cheek.

"I never want to see you again," she said in a low, determined voice.

"I would think it highly unlikely," he agreed, holding the door for her with exaggerated care.

A fresh feeling of despair washed over her, and more than anything she wished she could turn and fling herself into the dubious haven of his arms. She wanted to be back in that bed, in his arms, when none of this had happened. But, despite his protests, he didn't want her, not truly. And even if he did, his wife was in the next room. Without another word she swept from the room, head held high. She didn't look back as the door closed behind her with a quiet click.

# Chapter Twenty

IT WAS LATE afternoon a few days later. A light mist was falling, and Gillian took a moment out from her fevered packing to stare out into the London street.

"I don't see why you have to go so soon, Gilly," Felicity pouted from her perch in the center of the bed. "It's not as though Pamela were increasing again or anything like that. You could at least have waited for my wedding."

"Felicity, darling, we've been through this a thousand times or more. I'll be at your wedding in Sussex; I simply cannot stay in London and help you get ready for it."

"But why not?" Felicity wailed. "I don't know how I'll ever manage without you. Mother is completely helpless in matters like these. I was counting on you, Gilly."

"Well, you will simply have to count on yourself," she replied wearily, sorting through her clothes with reckless abandon. In one pile were all her prettiest frocks, with the brightest colors and most flattering lines. In the other was a pile of brown and gray stuff gowns better suited to a governess than a lady of independent means. It was the latter that was to be packed for her journey. "What will happen when you're a wife and mother, Felicity? You will have only yourself to fall back on then."

"Don't be absurd. When I have children I'll have you come and help me, just as you've done with Mother and the aunts," her niece replied saucily, unaware of the dread she was instilling in her favorite aunt's heart.

"Yes, very likely I will," she sighed gloomily.

"Must you leave tomorrow morning?" she begged. "If you could just put it off two more days then you could come with me and help me choose the materials for my trousseau. You know you have excellent taste and the best eye in London, or so Bertie assures me."

"No, thank you, my dear. But when you go you may return something for me."

"Something to Madame Racette's?" she inquired. "I didn't know anything she made up for you displeased you."

"I ordered it on an impulse, and have since regretted it," her aunt said shortly. "The dress is far too youthful for me."

Felicity bounced off the bed, knocking the folded clothing askew as she bounded over to the closet. "Oh, Gilly, is it this? I had no idea you actually bought it!" She held up the diaphanous aqua blue dress they had seen at Madame Racette's so long ago. "Have you ever worn it?"

"No, and I have no intention of doing so. It was mad of me to have bought it, and it would serve me right if she refused to accept it."

"Gilly, what is wrong?" Felicity questioned in a softer tone. "What happened? Has it something to do with Lord Marlowe? Bertie and I have been worried about you."

Picking up the tumbled clothes from the floor, Gilly placed a noncommittal expression on her face. "Well, thank you and Bertie for your concern, but there's absolutely nothing wrong. I am merely tired of the city. You know I prefer the country, and I miss Pamela."

"You can barely abide Pamela, and we both know it. Has he broken your heart?"

Gillian controlled her instinctive response, managing to sound cool. "My dear, ever since you and Liam have become betrothed you see everything from your own romantic viewpoint. My heart was never involved with Lord Marlowe, only my intellect. We are friends. No, we are acquaintances, and that is all. I don't expect we shall pursue the connection anymore."

"Then why did he send you gillyflowers?" her niece demanded wisely.

"How did you know it was he? I have other acquaintances, I may hope."

"You may hope so indeed, but I peeked at his card. Not that it said anything of interest. Just his name. I do wish you'd tell me what's going on. I do hate to be in the dark."

"You, my dear Felicity, are an incorrigible gossip, and I have no intention of gratifying your curiosity one whit." To her relief no gossip had arisen from her unfortunate visit to Marlowe's gaming club, at least not yet, and the sooner she was gone from London the less likely someone would connect her to that debacle.

"But why didn't you throw out the flowers if you're so angry with Lord Marlowe?"

"I didn't tell you I was angry with Lord Marlowe. I don't wish to discuss this any further, Felicity!"

"Miss Gillian!" Flossie tumbled into the room, her cheeks flushed. "There's someone here to see you."

Gillian's heart leaped inside her, and she took an involuntary step toward the door before she remembered. "Tell him I'm not at home," she replied dully.

"It's not a him, Miss Gillian. It's a her. A foreign lady, with a veil and a beautiful lilac cape. She says her name is Contessa Albini. Not that I hold much with them foreign titles, mind you. Shall I tell her you're not at home?"

Gillian had little doubt as to the identity of her caller, though why Helene should choose that unlikely title was more than she could fathom. It was the wrong time of day for social calls, so it could only be someone outside the ton. Which left Marlowe's wife.

She didn't want to see her. Didn't want to think of her again, but with her luck Helene Marlowe would camp out on her doorstep until she had her say. If she had come to commiserate over Marlowe's shabby treatment, Gillian thought she might scream.

"Tell her I'll be down," she said finally, peering into the mirror and smoothing her tumbled hair. Her blue eyes were hollowed by the sleepless nights, and her face looked alarmingly pale. It didn't matter—she could not compete with Helene's flamboyant beauty even at the best of times. "Is Letty downstairs?"

"No, miss."

"Just as well. I imagine we'll wish to talk in private."

"Who is this Contessa Albini?" Felicity demanded, all agog. "And why has she come to see you? I've never heard of the woman."

"None of your business, little one," Gilly said, keeping the sting from her voice. "You may assist by sorting through the rest of my clothes for me, and I'll be back in a short while."

Thus adjured, Felicity immediately began to reverse the piles of clothing, throwing the drab clothes under the bed with her usual abandon.

Helene rose from the damask-covered chair in the west salon as Gilly entered the room. She had removed the lilac veil, tossing it back over her midnight curls. In the dim twilight she looked even more beautiful than she had that night, with the shadows successfully hiding her age.

"I was hoping you wouldn't deny yourself," Helene greeted her frankly. "Though from what I've heard the last few days I wouldn't have blamed you. You haven't been treated very well, have you, my dear?"

Gilly ground her teeth as she shut the door behind her. "It's of little consequence."

"'Of little consequence,' she says! And I have had to spend the last three days listening to lamentations and ragings and threats and despair. It may be of no moment to you, my dear Gillian, but to others it is of great importance indeed. And me, I am not one to stand around and watch while others suffer. I take things into my own hands, and try my poor best to fix them up."

"I am certain you do, Contessa," Gilly replied, somewhat at a loss.

"Ronan would kill me with his bare hands if he knew I had come to plead his case. So would my husband. But me, I feel I owe Ronan something, and I decided this was the least I could do, and so I told poor Alfredo. Right now he is pacing his hotel room, wringing his hands, and he will be very angry with me when I return, no doubt. But I will manage him. I have always known how."

"I beg your pardon, Contessa. You have lost me. Who is Alfredo?"

"You must call me Helene! Indeed, I can never remember what my last name is. Alfredo is my husband, of course. The Count Albini."

"Your husband?" Gilly echoed. "But you said you were married to Marlowe."

"Well, I was. A great long time back. He was my second husband, and a very nice one he was, too, considering that we were never suited. He never held it against me, my little stratagems. However, he wasn't overly fond of Marco."

"Marco?" Gillian echoed.

"Marco was my third husband. Alfredo is my fourth. I had neglected to tell Ronan that I divorced him three years ago and decided it was time to remedy the situation."

"Then he isn't married?"

"Not to my knowledge. Unfortunately I have also had to give up the very generous allowance he has always made me, but then, Alfredo insisted. He is such a jealous sort." She surveyed a particularly fine diamond on her plump white hand with a fond sigh. "But I am forgetting myself. I have come to tell you about Ronan."

"Please, Contessa, there is no need." The last thing she wanted to hear was Ronan's former-wife trying to explain him.

"Helene, my dear. You must call me Helene. After all, we are to be in a way sisters-in-law, are we not?" she said obscurely. "And there is every need. My poor Ronan is in love with you."

"Don't be absurd. He has never loved anyone in his life," she shot back.

"You say that with a great deal of assurance, you who have known him scarcely a month, to a woman who was once his wife. He hasn't loved many people, not more than you can count on one hand. He loved his mother, and his grandmother, his reprobate Uncle George, and his blind and smelly old spaniel. And he loves you, my dear."

"What about you?" She allowed her curiosity to escape.

"No, he never loved me. You see, he might have, but I tricked him into marrying me. I told him I was pregnant, when many doctors have assured me that that dreadful prospect will never come to pass, and like a gentleman Ronan did the honorable thing. When he found out the truth he was perfectly polite. He already knew me rather well, and it came as no great surprise."

"I . . . I see," Gillian said lamely.

"I doubt that you do. Ronan is very sorry for the wager. Vivian has been having a bad influence on him, an influence I tried to warn him of years ago. But of course, being a man, he wouldn't listen. He does love you dearly."

"Vivian?"

"No, idiot! Ronan."

"How gratifying," she replied in icy tones.

"He has hurt you that much, *hein*?" Helene questioned sorrowfully. "He told me he had hurt you beyond bearing, but I know from experience that a woman in love will stand a great deal of hurting before the love dies."

"But I am not a woman in love, Helene."

"Are you not? I will take leave to doubt that also. I believe you love him as much as he loves you, and all this dillydallying is something I have little patience with."

"Then it is fortunate you will not have to put up with it. I am leaving for my sister's home in Winchester tomorrow, and Lord Marlowe can safely forget his guilty conscience."

"Ah, then it is a coward you are," the contessa said in a silken voice. "You could not face the thought of marrying a divorced man. I should have known . . . the British put such a great stock in their little rules of society."

"That has nothing to do with it. If Ronan loved me I would have lived with him without benefit of marriage. And he knows it."

"Would you really?" the contessa inquired, diverted. "Let me tell you, my dear, that is very unwise. You must always seek a wedding band first, or your future will in no way be assured. I tell you from my great experience that—"

"I have no intention of doing any such thing!" Gilly cried, exasperated.

"I do not understand what all this fuss is about," Helene sighed, rising. "It all comes down to two very simple facts: you love Ronan, Ronan loves you. And you have your silly pride, and Ronan has decided to be noble for a change and not ruin you by tying you to a divorced man. At least, not any more than he's already ruined you, of course, so you may both end your days being correct and noble and utterly alone. And I am completely out of patience with the both of you." Despite her sharp words she embraced Gilly in her scented arms. "If you want him, my dear, you will have to tell him so. Men are so very foolish, you understand." She kissed her wetly on both cheeks. "*Au revoir, chérie.* Doubtless I will see you again. In Paris, perhaps. Or Venice. The two of you may stay with Alfredo and me." With a wave of her scented handkerchief she departed, leaving Gilly staring after her wordlessly for a long moment. Lost in thought, she slowly returned to her bedroom.

Felicity was still in the middle of her bed. "I know who your mysterious visitor is!" she exclaimed triumphantly. "It must be Lord Marlowe's ex-wife."

Her aunt stared at her in shock. "How did you know he was married?" she demanded.

"Why, everyone knows. It's the latest on-dit. Apparently she's very beautiful and dreadfully vulgar. She's now married to a very handsome Italian nobleman half her age. No one seems to be holding it against Marlowe. Except, perhaps, you?" She eyed her aunt curiously.

"Me?" she echoed, her mind still dazed. "No, I don't hold his divorce against him."

"Then why are you so angry with him?" Felicity demanded with an air of great practicality.

Gillian sat down at her dressing table, staring at her flushed cheeks and reaching for her diamond earbobs. "I don't truly know," she murmured.

# Chapter Twenty-One

GILLIAN SURVEYED her room for one last time. There was no need for pillows in the bed to simulate her sleeping form, or lies to the servants about fictitious headaches. The Redfern family was out again, leaving Gillian to her final night in London and a good night's sleep. Or so they thought. When they returned home in the small hours of the morning, they would find their innocent trust misplaced. And the chicken would have flown the coop. Straight to the fox's lair.

Poor young Truffles did his best to look impassive when she reached the front door, though the sight of the clinging aqua silk must have unnerved him. "It's ten o'clock, miss."

"I know it, Truffles."

"Will you be wanting the carriage, miss?"

She smiled up at him sweetly as she drew her cape around her slender shoulders. "No, thank you. Lord Marlowe's house is just across the way. I'll walk."

"You'll be wanting me to accompany you, of course."

"No, thank you."

"But you'll be back shortly?" The poor boy was getting desperate.

"No, Truffles, I won't," she said serenely. "And I wish you might tell my brother so when you see him. Preferably tomorrow morning, but I'll leave it to your discretion." She pressed a small, heavy purse into his nerveless fingers. "You've been a good friend, Truffles. I'll be sorry to leave you."

"But, miss . . ." he protested miserably, not moving.

She reached out and opened the heavy oak door for herself. "Wish me luck, Truffles. I will need it." And she was gone into the London night.

It was a cool, crisp, clear evening. The stars shone very brightly in the inky sky, and Gillian could see her breath as she moved toward Bruton Street. With a sudden rush of superstition, she reached up and touched her diamond earbobs. The stones felt warm and alive in the cloud of hair, and she smiled, reassured.

The door was opened by the same poker-faced manservant who had granted her entrance not that many days ago. He viewed her arrival with an astonishing lack of surprise.

"Miss Redfern." Did his sepulchral voice sound faintly relieved? She couldn't be quite certain.

All her well-thought-out excuses fled as she stepped inside the magnificent hallway. "Ah . . . er . . ."

"Contessa Albini said we might expect you," the man-servant broke in smoothly, covering her embarrassment.

"She did, did she?" Gillian said wrathfully.

"We were all hoping she was correct. We've been extremely worried about the master, Miss Redfern."

"Why?" she asked bluntly, surrendering her cape to his expert hands.

"I've been with Master Ronan for most of his thirty-nine years, and I've never seen him laid so low. The sight of you would do wonders for him, I don't doubt. If he could see."

"What do you mean, if he could see?" she demanded, an absurd panic filling her. "You don't mean to say he's blind?"

"In a manner of speaking, miss. Shot the cat, he has, quite thoroughly."

"He *what?* Oh, I collect you mean he's drunk."

"Exactly, miss. Hasn't drawn a sober breath in the past three days. He's sound asleep, and I don't think anything short of Gabriel's trumpet could wake him right now."

"He's here? I had thought he would be at the gaming salon."

"Oh, no, miss. He gave that to Mr. Peacock."

"For heaven's sake, why?" She was growing more and more mystified.

"He said it was a farewell present. Master Vivian has been hanging on his coattails for I don't know how long, ever since they were boys together, and a nasty piece of goods he is. I tried to warn his lordship, but he'd hear none of it. He's always been the loyal sort. I suppose he finally decided to heed my warnings."

"Could you . . . could you show me to his room?" There was no way she could request such an outrageous thing without blushing deeply, but the manservant was too well trained to indicate that he noticed. She searched her brain for his name and came up with it triumphantly after a moment. "If it wouldn't be too much trouble, Mr. Watkins?"

A beam reflected his appreciation of her memory. "Just Watkins is good enough for the likes of me, miss. And I'd be honored to do so. If you'll follow me."

Gillian wasn't as surprised by the sparse nature of Marlowe's sleeping chamber as her niece had been before her. Indeed, her attention was more caught up by the occupant of the large bed than the furnishings.

He lay on his back, one arm flung out to one side, black hair rumpled across his high forehead. He was still dressed, although someone, presumably Watkins, had removed his coat and cravat and undone the snowy linen shirt. His boots were lying at the foot of the bed, and a thin blanket covered his powerful frame. She looked at him, and the one thing she wanted to do was strip off her clothes and curl up next to him. She stayed where she was, her face impassive.

"He won't wake up, miss," Watkins said in a normal tone of voice. "He's a three-bottle man, but it's been closer to eight, and he sleeps like the dead until it wears off. I don't expect to see any signs of life from him until morning."

"It's just as well," Gilly sighed, surveying the meager furniture scattered around the room. "Could you help me move that chair, Watkins?"

"Where to, miss?"

"Just to the side of the bed. And if you could perhaps find me a foot stool and a blanket. And then I should be quite comfortable."

Watkins's impassivity deserted him. "Are you planning to stay, miss?" he asked, agog.

"I am. That is, if you have no objections."

"None in the slightest, miss. His lordship couldn't ask for a better lady. Nor you a finer gentleman, when all's said and done," he added staunchly.

That remained to be seen. He'd said he'd loved her, and she hadn't believed him. She was taking a desperate chance on the possibility that he really did, and if she was wrong—well, things couldn't get much worse.

She smiled her sweet, unaffected smile that had made more than one susceptible male her slave. "I know it," she said gently, stealing a glance at her besotted love.

Ten minutes later Gillian was comfortably ensconced, a stool under her feet, a lambswool blanket around her, a glass of excellent brandy in her hand. During all the bother Marlowe had scarcely stirred, only muttering an imprecation under his breath when they piled another blanket on top of his sleeping frame.

"You're sure you'll be all right, miss?" Watkins asked anxiously on his way out the door. The fire was nicely built up, sending a warm glow through the room. "If you want, you need only ring. I could find you a bedroom if you'd just say the word."

"No, I think it would be better if I stayed right where I am. But thank you, Watkins. I'm sure I'll be very comfortable."

Half an hour later she wasn't so sure. Despite the dulling effects of the brandy she was still wound up, and the hairpins were digging into her tender scalp, giving her a wretched headache. She took them out, shaking her tawny hair loose about her shoulders in an impatient gesture, when another sound came from Marlowe. A whisper, so quiet she couldn't make it out, followed by another.

Abandoning her blanket, she got to her stocking feet and edged closer to the bed. He was still sound asleep, albeit more restlessly so than before. He tossed and turned, muttering something over and over again. Tentatively she put one knee on the high bed, moving closer to catch his words. It was with a start that she recognized her own name coming from his dreaming lips, and in a tone of longing that sent tears to her eyes.

He looked years younger and curiously vulnerable in sleep. She longed to reach out and smooth his brow. Even more, she longed to curl up on the soft mattress beside him and sleep. It was a big enough bed; surely he was too far gone to notice.

He turned again, flinging an arm toward her, and reluctantly she climbed down off the bed. It would be the better part of valor to stay in her chair that night. Much as she regretted the necessity, it wouldn't do to take advantage of the man.

Almost as if he knew the fevered thoughts that passed through her mind, Marlowe muttered another oath, then turned and began to snore. Gilly laughed aloud, feeling cheered. There was something so homely and prosaic about snoring. Something so very wifely about hearing it. She settled back into her far from comfortable chair with a happy sigh.

A quiet knock on the door awoke her. The first light of dawn was streaking in the windows, the fire was burned down to a few embers, and Marlowe was still in a state of advanced insensibility. She moved around the bed to the door and was assailed by the heavenly odor of coffee before she reached it. She opened it a crack and discovered Watkins, a tray in his hands.

"Is he awake yet, miss?" he inquired in a whisper.

"Not yet."

"He always wants his coffee when he does. I didn't dare not bring it.

Would you be caring for some tea?"

"Coffee will be splendid. If you would bring another cup for his lordship."

"Yes, miss. Shall I build up the fire for you?"

"I'll take care of it. Tell me, is he . . . bad-tempered when he wakes up? I mean, after a night such as last night?"

"Gloomy's more like it. Then he gets his coffee and a huge breakfast and feels more the thing. Though he hasn't the last few days. You've given him a nasty turn, miss, that you have."

Good, she thought. "Well, let us hope I can cheer him up."

He still hadn't moved when she re-entered the bedroom. Setting the tray on the table beside her chair, she moved quietly to build up the fire. It was just after she had coaxed a tentative flame from the stubborn coals that she felt his eyes upon her narrow back. She fiddled with the wood a moment longer to give herself time to regain a modicum of self-possession, then rose and moved gracefully back to her chair, meeting his astonished eyes with perfect calm.

"Would you care for some coffee, my lord?" she inquired pleasantly, pouring a cup.

"What in God's name are you doing here?" he demanded by way of a greeting.

She took a sip out of the steaming brew and smiled at him. "Drinking your coffee."

"Don't be pert. How long have you been here?"

"Since ten o'clock last night. And, I can't help being pert. I feel pert this morning."

Marlowe shut his eyes and groaned. "Where did you sleep?"

"In this chair. And I must say it was not terribly comfortable. Watkins offered to find me a bed, but I told him I would be better off here."

"Why?"

Setting down the coffee, she climbed up onto the big bed and drew her legs underneath her aqua skirts, staring at him out of solemn eyes. "So that I can be well and truly compromised, of course," she explained simply, as if to a child. "No one seems to realize I spent the night in your bed just a few days ago, so I thought I'd better make sure that this relatively innocent night doesn't go unremarked."

The dark eyes flew open to stare at her once more. "I spent a great deal of money to ensure your reputation was intact! Does your family know you're here?" he demanded grimly.

"They do by now. I shouldn't doubt I've been cast off completely." The prospect didn't seem to daunt her.

"And what put this clever idea into your brain?"

"Felicity, of course. If she had enough bottom to secure the man she loved, then I could at least do my best. It would be extremely foolish to let missishness get in the way of our future happiness."

"Our future happiness?" he echoed hollowly, and Gilly felt a pang of dismay. His reaction so far had not been promising. "I gathered last time we met that you hated me."

"Well, to be perfectly frank, there are times that I do hate you. That wager was perfectly hateful of you, and well you know it."

"I told you I deeply regretted it . . ." He winced as his voice got louder.

"I know you did. And I decided to take you at your word. You also told me that you loved me."

"Gilly." He sat up and caught her hand in his. "I'm a divorced man. You haven't thought it out clearly."

"Better a divorced man than a married one," she observed with a charming practicality. "And I am a ruined woman. If you won't have me, I suppose I could always set up housekeeping on my own. Though Felicity tells me she expects me to run her household and bring up her children when the time comes. I don't know what Liam will say to that, but—"

"No!"

"Well, I rather think he'd say so, too," she confided. "But then, Felicity has a way about her."

"*I* say no." He pulled her closer. "You've spent far too much of your life taking care of other women's families."

"Yes, I rather agree. I would like children of my own, please. If it's not too much trouble."

"Gilly . . ."

"And you don't even have to marry me. I don't blame you for feeling cynical after marrying someone like Helene, and if you'd prefer to live in sin I would understand completely."

"There's no comparison between you and Helene," he said roughly.

"No, she's a great deal prettier," Gilly said calmly.

"She's a heartless jade."

"And what am I, dear Ronan?" Gilly inquired, the light in his green eyes making her suddenly more sure of herself. She reached out and smoothed the tumbled lock of hair from his high forehead.

He pulled her unresisting body into his arms, and she nestled comfortably against his broad chest. The warmth of him, the scent of him, the feel of him brought everything back, and she wanted nothing more than to strip off her clothes and crawl beneath him. "You, my dear, are an incorrigible minx." She felt his lips on her cloud of hair, and she breathed a deep sigh of relief. His arms tightened around her possessively.

After a long moment he spoke. "Is it to be Gretna Green or a special license?"

She pulled herself out of his arms. "You don't really have to marry me, you know," she said earnestly.

"I most certainly do. I intend to chain you to me through every stratagem known to man and law. You'll marry me, my girl, whether you like it or not. There'll be no more debauchery until we're wed in the sight of God and man."

"I would like it very much, thank you." Her voice was deceptively meek. "Which would be faster? I'd really like to be debauched again."

He laughed, cupping her face to kiss her. "I am owed a few favors. I could likely get a special license by this afternoon, and it would take us days to get to Scotland." He pulled her back into the comforting haven of his arms. "Unless, of course, you'd prefer a formal wedding."

"With Derwent to give me away and Letty and the others as my attendants?" she inquired with a laugh. "The idea tempts me, but I feel I must decline. Unless, of course, you have a sudden longing for a horde of Redferns on your doorstep?"

"Unless I get moving shortly, I am very likely to suffer that very fate." He stayed right where he was, his arms tight around her slender body. "Do you mind very much if I turn over a new leaf?"

"What did you have in mind?"

"No gambling, or late hours, or city lights, or wenching."

She struggled to sit up. "What, no wenching?" she exclaimed. "But what about me?"

"Only Gillian-wenching," he promised. "And you must make similar promises."

"That is quite easy. I promise not to gamble or to go wenching either."

"No, my dear. You must wear your hair unbound, go without shoes, and be rude to all your family."

"That, dear Ronan, should be extraordinarily easy." She sank gratefully back into his arms.

# About the Author

Anne Stuart recently celebrated her forty years as a published author. She has won every major award in the romance field, and appeared on the bestseller list of the NYTimes, Publisher's Weekly, and USA Today, as well as being featured in Vogue, People Magazine, and Entertainment Tonight. Anne lives by a lake in the hills of Northern Vermont with her fabulous husband.

CPSIA information can be obtained
at www.ICGtesting.com
Printed in the USA
LVOW11s0253140317
527047LV00001B/254/P